October

Chapter 1:   Sharon

"You got me pregnant!" I blurted at Doc.

Doc gasped, and her eyes grew in size. "Well! Good afternoon to you, Sharon! How are you doing?" Doc greeted me. I've been coming to Dynamic Health and Wellness Center for a long time now. I love my chiropractor! I love coming to get adjusted! It has kept me moving and doing the things I love to do.

My name is Dr. Sharon Lyle. I am the chairperson of the Biology department at Gateway Community College. I am also a newlywed. I married my college sweetheart, Anthony Lyle, just a little over a year ago.

"Perhaps I could have started with 'good afternoon'. Let me do that over. Good afternoon, Doc. You got me pregnant! I'm doing ok. How are you?" I excitedly replied. Doc did not get me pregnant in the conventional sense, but she helped me get pregnant.

"I'm doing great!" she said. Then she continued, "So, that fatigue was related to my suspicion? You are pregnant?!"

About three weeks ago when I came in to get adjusted, Doc noticed some changes to what she calls 'my baseline presentation.' The way she explained it to me was, there is a general posture I have when I come in based on the lifestyle I live. So, there are certain areas she just expect to need treatment. On this particular day, my body had some new areas that needed to be addressed. She had said, *"Sharon, how's the married life treating you?"* I had answered, *"Great"*, while preparing to lie face down on the chiropractic table. She began examining me. She checked my hips, then my low back. Before continuing upward, she paused, and said, *"Humor me. Before I say what I am going to say next, let me just say as a disclaimer: I'm speculating, but may be spot on. Are you and your husband trying to have a baby?"* For some reason, the hair on the back on my neck stood straight up. *"Yes. Why?"* I had answered. She said, *"There are changes in your pelvis and low back that suggest you may be pregnant."* I whipped my head around really quickly to look over my shoulder at Doc in disbelief. There is no way she can tell that. Is it? My mind began to flood with questions. Before I knew it, they were spewing forth with rapid speed. *"How can you tell that? What did my body say that points to pregnancy? How could my body possibly show that when it just happened a few days ago? Are you doing voodoo?"*

Doc laughed; and understandably so. My exaggerated facial expressions can be quite comical. I mean, I can be quite a character. Simply stated, I was amazed. I am often amazed at how well she can decode my body. Once Doc caught her breath from laughing, she began to answer my questions.

"Sharon, when you come in for an adjustment, I usually only have to adjust one particular area of your hip and a couple of segments in your lower back. Well, today, I had to adjust your pubic bone and a specific part of your lower back. Now, you are wondering 'how does that translate to pregnancy.' Right?" she said.

I answered, *"Um, yes."*

"There is a specific spinal level in your back that affects your reproductive organs, such as your uterus. If this was the only finding, I would not have suspected pregnancy. I would have asked about changes in your menstrual cycle. It was the changes in the pelvis that made me suspect pregnancy. The joints in your pelvis and hips had all shifted because of a hormone that is released upon conception. This hormone relaxes the ligaments in a woman's body to prepare the body for the growth of a fetus." Nothing else was said for a few moments. Doc was allowing me those moments of silence to process all that she had said.

Once again, I must say, I was stunned. By the time she had finished her explanation, I had sat up on the table. It was a little difficult to take that kind of information lying down. Finally, I said, *"But, it has only been, what? Three days?! I remember exactly when it happened. And you are telling me ALL of that has happened?"* Doc simply nodded, yes. What else was there left for me to say? Nothing. So, I turned to lie face down on the table again to finish getting adjusted.

After that visit, I eventually took a pregnancy test. The test was positive, and I was definitely pregnant.

"Yeah. So, about your speculations. Yes, I am pregnant! We are expecting a baby!" I said.

Doc smiled, and said, "Congratulations!" Then, her expression became serious. "Just because I told you I thought you were pregnant before you took the test, please do not advertise to people I can tell if you are pregnant before a missed period. I was able to guess it because I know what *'normal'* is for YOU."

"I understand," I said. "By the way, I have a confession to make."

"What's that?" she answered.

"Although my husband and I are very excited about our pregnancy, we are both very nervous. This is not our first pregnancy. We were pregnant once while we were engaged. Sadly, we lost the baby early on. We don't want to lose another baby. We really want a family," I said.

"Sharon, when did you lose the baby? Was it before or after you became my patient?" Doc asked.

"It was just before I came here." I answered.

"If you recall, it was your chronic low back pain that brought you in, and one of the things I uncovered during your exam was your irregular periods. The nerve root that affects your periods can also play a role in miscarriages. Since you've been getting adjustments, your cycle is regular, minus all the painful cramping and heavy flow. Continued care will help increase the chances of a healthy mommy and baby." she said.

I took a deep breath and sighed. Doc soothingly rubbed her hand across my upper back to let me know she understood. After another moment of silence, she continued with the rest of my adjustment.

Feeling a whole lot calmer and less achy after my adjustment, I stood up and gave Doc a hug. "Thank you so much. I appreciate all that you do."

"You are very welcome. Before you leave, Sharon, please advise that I will see you in four weeks unless you are feeling like you need an adjustment sooner. If you are feeling achy just call and get on the schedule," she said.

"Ok", I replied, and began gathering my purse.

"And, lastly, will you be at the retreat?" she asked.

"I sure will be at the retreat! I have heard so much about this retreat. There is no way I am going to miss it. It will be a great way to unwind and get away." Turning to walk down the hall, I called over my shoulder, "See you in a few days."

As I approached the front office, I could hear someone talking to Anthony about the retreat.

"Man, I'm telling you! It is so much fun! You will DEF-initely have a great time! The food is delicious, the workshops are entertaining, educational, and hands-on. The scenery is gorgeous, especially at sunset. It's a great opportunity to network, too. Patients are allowed to bring one guest. So you meet new people and build relationships. Oh! And you get to try new things like horseback riding. You should definitely go on the retreat. It's like a mini vacay", said the man sitting to the left of my husband. I don't know who the man was. This was the first time I had ever seen him in the office.

I walked over to my husband. Once I was standing beside him, my husband looked up at me, and said, "So, what do you think about this retreat they are trying to convince me to attend?"

Trying to play down my excitement, I shrugged and responded, "Personally, I'm looking forward to it."

Anthony smiled while shaking his head at me. He read right through my act, "Why am I not surprised?" Standing up, he asked, "Are you ready to leave?"

I leaned in to kiss him on the lips, and said, "Yes." I was grinning from ear to ear. I smiled at Doc's assistant, and waved goodbye. He returned the wave and said, "Let's get your appointment scheduled before you go."

While I scheduled my next appointment, Anthony extended his right hand to the man for a handshake, "It was nice to meet you, Sean."

"Same here," he said.

"Good afternoon, Sean", Doc greeted me. "You are looking really good. I can tell you have truly cleaned up your diet." I have been coming to Doc for a while. Before I became a patient here, I had not too long before learned how unhealthy I was.

My name is Sean Struthers. I am a Financial Aid Officer at Gateway State University. I sit at my desk, process student loans, and keep track of payments. In my college years, I was an All American Athlete, and in the best shape of my life. After college, I dated a sous chef for a couple of years. Man, did she love to feed me. When she was not at work, her favorite thing to do was sit at home and watch movies. She cooked; we ate, and watched movies. The sedentary life took its toll. I gained over forty pounds within a couple of months. I found myself overweight, diagnosed with high blood pressure, and a borderline diabetic. I also started noticing self – esteem issues. My girlfriend must have noticed too, because she became verbally abusive. The verbal abuse was subtle and infrequent at first. Then, it become constant. That was my cue to exit stage left. Some may argue, I should have left long before that point, but I was blinded by love. Leaving her was the hardest thing to do, but one of the best decisions I made.

When I left her, I decided to cleanse myself and work on me. I started going to the gym. I was lifting weights, jogging, and eating better. I ditched the pork, and eventually the beef, and began loading up on fruits, vegetables, mixed nuts, and more importantly, WATER! I had also began meditating daily, assessing my goals in life, and determining what kind of person I wanted to become.

I had been single for about a year before I met the love of my life, Lisa. She was like a breath of fresh air. She was encouraging, full of life, and fun. At first, she was intimidating to me, because I had never met a woman who did not need me, but wanted me; a woman who didn't want to complete me, but compliment me. One of the reasons she was so happy, confident, and full of life was because she stayed active. She exercised four to five times a week, and went on long bike rides over the weekend. I could not keep up with her at that time, but I longed to. She gave me life!

As we became better friends, I fell in love. I had fallen in love with my friend.

"Yes, I have been doing really well with my lifestyle changes. I'm also doing great as far as my back is concerned. I don't have the continuous ache throughout the whole back. Now, the pain is off and on." I answered before lying on the table for my treatment. Although I am being treated for back pain, it is not the initial back pain I came in with. I have long since healed from that injury. However, recently, I hurt my back again doing something foolish. I decided to try out the hoover board one of my nephews got for his birthday. The hoover board came from under me and I found myself lying on my back and looking up at the ceiling. Hurt.

"Wonderful! Let's get your blood pressure," Doc said. She places the cuff on my arm and hits the button on the machine. The cuff squeezed tightly on my upper arm for about fifteen seconds or so, and then released. "One fifteen over seventy-six. Keep up the good work! What has your medical doctor had to say?"

"She has taken me off the blood pressure medicine, which I am so happy about. Plus, Lisa and I have talked about growing our family. So, that's what we are working on now." I excitedly shared with Doc.

"That's great news! I wish you all the best." After making a few notes in my chart, Doc asked, "Will you and Lisa be at the retreat this weekend?"

"We wouldn't miss it for the world." I said as I stood up from the table.

"Very good. I look forward to seeing you there," she said before I walked out of the treatment room.

Lisa and I were super excited about this retreat. This will be our first retreat together as a couple. We both have attended the retreat before, but never in the same year or as a couple.

Chapter 3: Jennifer

"Did you pack everything into the car that I had sitting near the door?" I asked my guy of three years. Mark and I met while visiting the Missouri History Museum. I was heading into the Little Black Dress exhibit with some girlfriends. We were having a girls' day out. Mark was behind me, heading towards another exhibit. This particular day was the opening day for the Little Black Dress. So, there were a lot of visitors moving about the corridor. In the brief moment that he had looked down at a brochure in his hand, the flow of traffic abruptly stopped. Since he was not paying attention, he bumped into me hard, from behind, nearly knocking me to the floor. Noticing that I was getting ready to fall, he dropped the brochure, and quickly and firmly, grabbed me by my waist to catch me. His brochure fell, and so did my crutches. One crutch fell to the floor, uninterrupted, but the other crutch hit another lady on its way down.

Hearing the commotion, my friend Martha turned around to see what all the ruckus was. Seeing my crutches on the floor, she made her way over to us, gathering my crutches on the way. She also eyeballed Mark, who was still holding me close to him with his arm around my waist. Never taking her gaze off of him, she handed me the crutches. Although I reached for them and began shifting my weight onto them, Mark was slow to let me go.

"Please, forgive me for my carelessness." He said in a baritone voice. "Are you ok?" Before I responded, I turned around to face him. I wanted to see who had knocked me over. Let me just say, I was not prepared for the sight in front of me. He was tall, muscular, with smooth dark chocolate skin that created a high contrast against the pearly whites he had flashed at me.

Once I found my voice, I responded, "I'm ok. Thank you." Silently, I was wishing he would wrap his arms around me again. "What's your name?" I asked.

Extending his right hand, he said, "I'm Mark. And, yours?"

"I'm Jennifer. Nice to meet you, although I wish it were under better circumstances." I smiled at him; Martha glared at him.

Mark smiled once more before excusing himself and walking past. His arm brushed my bare arm. It happened very quickly. I can't quite explain it, but I felt an energy transfer between us. I watched him make his way over to the stairwell that led upstairs to the past and current events of St. Louis. Man, was he a sight for sore eyes! When he had finally disappeared in one of the galleries, I turned my attention to Martha.

"What was that all about," she asked. I recounted the events to her, and she simply shook her head and told me to come on because everyone was waiting for us.

The Little Black Dress exhibit was amazing! I had no idea there were different dresses for each stage of mourning or for whom you were mourning. I enjoyed the exhibit so much that I had temporarily forgotten all about Mark. That is, until I saw him again as we were walking towards the front of the museum. We were walking past the Fair St. Louis exhibit hall when I spotted him. Heading towards me, he smiled and waved at me, indicating to me to wait up. I told my girlfriends to give me a moment. They did.

It did not take long for Mark to cover the distance between us. Once again, he flashed me that beautiful smile.

Standing in front of me, he asked, "Jennifer, right?"

"Yes. Mark, is it?" I answered. This time, he blushed. How cute! Although he looked to be in his late 50's, maybe early 60's, his smile gave him a boyish look.

"Jennifer, do you mind if I call you sometime? There is something about you, and I can't shake it. I want to get to know you."

I was flattered and pleasantly surprised! Mark was clearly about twelve years my junior. But hey! I definitely did not mind. I don't really want to be bothered with an old man. We exchanged numbers and the rest was history. Three years later, we were still making each other happy.

Today, he was driving me to my chiropractor's office to board the charter bus that would take me and many others down to the boot heel for a weekend retreat. As a patient of Doc's, I could have brought a guest. If I had, it would have been Mark, but he had another event to attend. Besides, we could use this time to take a break from each other; make us miss one another.

As we pulled into the parking lot, we could see the bus driver loading bags underneath the bus. Mark parked the car behind the bus and turned on his double flashers. He popped the trunk from a button on the floor board. He removed my bags from the trunk, and took my crutches out of the backseat; laying them against the car. He opened my door, and said, "I'm going to take your bags over to the bus first. Then, I will help you out of the car." I waited patiently in the car until he returned. As soon as he got back to the car, he held his hand out to help me stand. Then, he handed me the crutches he had resting against the car. Once I had balanced myself on my crutches, Mark stepped up to me and wrapped his arms around my waist. "I'm going to miss you, Love," he said.

I leaned into him, and stretched my face upwards for a kiss. "I'm going to miss you, too." Just as I began making my way towards the bus, I stopped, and turned back to Mark. "I'm also going to miss those work boots." His eyes became hooded. He dropped his chin and his tone became sultry.

"You know I keep those work boots by the bed just for you. We are going to put in work when you return." I blew him a kiss, and then continued onto the line that was forming to board the bus. The line moved rather quickly. So, I didn't have to wait long.

Mark looked on from the car. He watched me disappear onto the bus, but he did not drive off immediately. He waited until the bus drove out of the parking lot.

When the last rider boarded the bus and took a seat, the driver boarded. He grabbed the mic from the walkie talkie radio to make an announcement. "Hello, everyone! Welcome aboard! My name is Sterling, and I am your bus driver. Please get as comfortable as you can. It is now a little after 10:00 a.m. We should arrive in Atlanta by 8:00 p.m." he said. He had barely finished speaking when a couple of riders loudly exclaimed, "Atlanta?! I'm on the wrong bus", while others laughed at the joke. "I'm just kidding! We'll be in Potosi in a couple of hours," he laughed, and then sat down to drive.

As we pulled out of the parking lot, Mark followed. The bus turned one way; Mark turned the opposite way. During the two hour drive down, I thought about those boots. I could not wait to get back to my work boots.

Chapter 4: Kelly

The bus pulled out of the parking lot, and eased into traffic. I watched as familiar buildings passed the window until we merged onto highway 55. That was the last I saw before I fell asleep. I always fall asleep on road trips. If you want someone to keep you company on the road, I am not the one.

About an hour later, *'Where in the hell?'* was the first thought that came to mind when I saw the "Welcome to Potosi: Population 2,684". My second thought was, *'Um is any other black person feeling slightly uncomfortable rolling through this hick town in the southern part of Missouri?"*

My name is Kelly Jackson, and I am heading to a place called Clear Water Lodge. I was invited on a retreat by my best friend, Nina. Nina is a patient of a chiropractor who hosts annual weekend retreats for her patients and their guests. These retreats are supposed to be all the rave. Nina has been on this retreat before and she enjoyed it so much that she insisted that I come to the next one with her. Thus, I am on this bus riding through this town that looks like something out of an old movie.

This year, the theme of the weekend is Creating Your Inner Peace: How to Destress Your Life. Let Nina tell it, she can sense my lack of inner peace. Um, whatever. She thinks she knows me. Ok, well, maybe she does. Nina and I met in grade school. We are products of the Gateway City Public School district. After high school, we attended vastly different colleges. I attended a Historically Black College/University down south, and she attended a Predominantly White College in the Midwest. I work for a major telecommunications company in St. Louis and she works for the federal government and teaches at the community college. Despite our wildly different paths, we have remained the best of friends. I love her to pieces. She is my sister from another mother.

"Nina, wake up. We are here." I gently nudged my friend awake. At some point after I had fallen asleep, so had she; softly snoring. I would not even be surprised if she had been drooling. The trip was just under two hours long, but Nina looks like she has been sleeping for four hours. "Tired much?" I asked.

On the other side of this small town, the bus continued onto a two lane highway for another twenty minutes; passing several farms on the way. At a T-intersection, the driver made a left onto another winding two lane road that brought us to the entrance of a tree lined drive leading to Clear Water Lodge. When the bus pulled up in front of the main lodge and parked, everyone stood up to stretch. Then, they all filed off the bus and gathered on the sidewalk where we patiently waited for our bags to be unloaded from beneath the bus, and for Doc to bring the keys and cabin assignments.

Clear Water Lodge was actually a very serene location. I could feel a calmness blanketing over me. Behind the main lodge was the lake for which it was named. The sun was shining brightly, and there was a slight chill in the October air. I closed my eyes, raised my face to the sky, and inhaled. "So, this is what clean air smells like?" I said to Nina without opening my eyes. Suddenly, I felt something tickle my nose. Still, without opening my eyes, I swatted. Then, I felt something touch my forehead. I swatted again. This time, I opened my eyes. Something flew directly towards my eyes. I swatted at it to avoid being hit by it. It doubled back past my face and landed on my arm. I looked down to see a lady bug on my arm. Just as I was getting ready to say, "Aww, a lady bug", several more began flying around me. They were everywhere! A few feet away from me, a woman was swatting and trying to dodge the swarm of lady bugs.

"Yes. I love it", Nina replied, as she too, swatted at the lady bugs. Tapping me on my left arm, she said, "Our bags are ready." I had been too busy knocking the lady bugs away that I did not notice that all of the bags had been unloaded   from the bus. There were several small piles of carry-on bags and totes. We grabbed ours, and stood off to the side to wait for Doc.

Doc exited the lodge behind us with an envelope full of keys and a roster. "Ladies and gentlemen, I have your lodging assignments and keys. Here in the main lodge behind me, we have Nina Scott and Kelly Jackson in Guest Room number three one four. Lisa Struthers and Sharon B. Lyle, you are also in the lodge and in Guest Room number twenty-two. Sean Struthers, Stephen Jones, Anthony Lyle, and Marcus Thymes are in the Lakeview Family Cabins", said Doc. She continued calling off the rooms until she was done. After hearing which room we were in, neither Nina or I paid attention to Marcus' name being called. Our minds were set on getting to the room. We already had the itinerary, which was given to us when we boarded the bus at the office. So, we knew when and where we were expected.

We walked through the front entrance of the lodge into a large open room. To our left was a grand fireplace with a fire burning. On each side of the fireplace were two oversized chaise, with a knitted throw over the backs. Behind the chaises was a coffee table with a bowl of apples and oranges and a few magazines about the great outdoors. Along the wall on the same side as the entrance was a table with two chairs and a checkers' game board on top. To our right was the media center. There was an eight foot long table with three computer monitors on one end of the table. The other side was for people who wanted to plug in their own devices. In front of us was the long welcome counter where Doc checked in.

The young girl, who looked like she was in high school, smiled and said, "Hello, Ladies! Welcome to Clear Water Lodge. All of the meeting rooms will be down this hallway to your left. If you need any assistance, don't hesitate to let us know." I was surprised she was an African American.

Nina and I nodded and thanked her for her assistance before heading towards the elevator. We waited for the elevator. Since there were only four floors in the main lodge, it did not take terribly long for it to arrive to the first floor. This was such a small old elevator. The one door to the elevator slid opened to the left. I entered the elevator first; then Nina. It was so small, that there was only room for one more person and a rolling carry-on. The people behind us decided to just wait for the elevator to return instead of joining us.

On the third floor, Nina got off first. Ahead of me by several paces, she arrived at our room quickly. When she reached the door to our room, she slid the key card into the slot above the handle and waited for the four green lights to appear. She pressed the handle downward and then, pushed it open. Once inside the room, she held the door open for me to follow.

"This is so nice. I thought we were going to be in a log cabin like Little House on the Prairie, or something. This is sort of like an old hotel. Nice", I said to Nina once we were inside our room.

"There are various cabin styles here. It's just that we are in the hotel-style rooms. The guys are in the cabin cabins", she answered. "I really love coming here. There is one major drawback; there is no cellphone reception down here. Well, maybe I should say spotty reception. The same drawback is also the appeal to this place."

While she spoke, I surveyed the room. I walked over to the window and opened the curtains. We had an awesome view of the lake. The sun was beginning to set, and it looked beautiful over the lake. "This is breathtaking, Nina."

"It sure is", she answered. She removed the itinerary from her purse and flipped through the retreat packet until she found what she was looking for. Sitting down on the edge of the bed, she said, "We have about 45 minutes until the Meet and Greet/Welcome starts. I guess I will freshen up a little."

Since the meeting rooms were all located in the lodge where we were staying, we did not have to walk far.

'This is Sean. Leave a message.' This was the third time I had called since leaving St. Anthony's Hospital. After work, I had stopped by the hospital to visit my cousin, Shannon, and her new baby girl. I had promised her I would come see her before I left for the weekend. Shannon and I are very close, and have been since were very little. She came to live with my mom and me after her mother passed away.

The first time I called Sean, I had been standing at the elevators, waiting for one to arrive to the floor. The call went straight to voicemail. So, I sent a text message. It took several seconds longer than usual for the "delivered" notification to appear. That means Sean is in an area without reception. I shrugged it off.

Once I had gotten to the lobby of the hospital, I tried calling him again; and again, it went straight to voicemail. I ended the call and put the Lodge's address into the phone's GPS. The fastest route said it will take me about one and a half hours from here. I looked at my watch. It was just after 11:30 a.m. There was more foot traffic in the lobby than it had been when I had first arrived a couple of hours ago. Medical personnel were bustling towards the cafeteria. Visitors were entering the hospital and going in all directions. Some went towards the elevators, while some went into the grand gift shop.

The October sun was shining brightly through the sliding door entrance of the hospital. Therefore, I put on my shades, and exited the hospital. My motorcycle was parked on the first row. So, I did not have far to walk. During the walk, I tried calling Sean again. Still, straight to voicemail. I put my Bluetooth headset on, placed my cell phone in my pocket, and donned my helmet.

Looking at the odometer, I read a half of tank of gas. That is plenty of gas to make it there, but I wanted to fill up anyway. I always fill up before hitting the road. There was a QT down the road. When I pulled up to the small QT, there were only a few other vehicles at the pumps

I dismounted my bike, and turned to the pumps. I swiped my card, and grabbed the pump to begin fueling my bike. While it fueled, I turned to observe the scenery around me. There wasn't much to take in, and there were only two other vehicles there besides mine. Behind me, the pump clicked, signaling that my tank was full. I hung the nozzle back up, pulled my helmet back on, mounted my bike, and revved the engine.

According to GPS, I was about twelve minutes away from highway 21, which would take me to Potosi. I love taking road trips this time of year. The scenery is very beautiful; the orange, red, and yellow leaves on the trees, the crisp air, and the open road.

Highway 21 was a hilly, winding, narrow, two-lane road. Yet, the speed limit read 55 mile per hour. There was no wonder why there were signs on the road saying "Make 21 Safer". I had a few suggestions, like widen the road. But, what do I know?

I rode through Hillsboro, and Desoto. As I rode pass one house, a boxer on a very long leash gave me a start! His leash allowed him enough free range to reach all the way to the edge of the road. As I drove by, he jumped and barked at me. I swerved towards the dotted yellow line in the middle of the road. Luckily, I was the only vehicle on the road at the time. Just as quickly, I corrected my bike and continued on my drive. My heartrate eventually came down.

Thirty minutes later, I came to a stoplight. It was hard to follow the directions on the GPS, because the directions were not very clear, and the street name was not visible. Highway 21 took a hard right and a quick left, and continued in a different direction. I didn't realize this until I had missed the turn. The GPS re-routed and took me a different way without instructing me to turn around. Less than fifteen minutes later, I was entering what looks like the center of town. It looked like something out of an old movie. This was definitely Small Town, USA.

My motorcycle attracted many stares, but I continued on. On the other side of town, there was more open country. According to GPS, I was another fifteen minutes out.

"Call Sean", I told Siri.

'Calling Sean.' She responded.

The phone began to ring in my headset. The phone rang one good time, then it went straight to voicemail.

"Damn, Sean! Answer the phone. I don't know where I am heading." I said as I ended the call before the voicemail greeting finished.

I covered the last few miles quicker than the fifteen minutes predicted by the GPS. I must admit, that was my goal. Surely, the time expectation is merely a challenge to the driver to beat that expected time of arrival. Right?

'The destination is on your left.'

'Arrived.' The GPS said.

I saw the sign to the right of the drive way that read **Clear Water Lodge**. I turned in. The drive was a rocky covered road with trees lining both sides. A few birds flew overhead as I cleared a canopy over the road. I came to a fork in the road. The arrow directed me to the right; so I took the road on the right. I followed the road until I came out alongside a lake. Looking at the lake, I can tell it was the inspiration for the name of the lodge. Across from the lake were several cabins. Visitors were entering and leaving them while engaging in conversations. I kept driving, expecting to eventually see the visitors' center or something. Instead, I came to a circular drive that ended nowhere. Ok. Now, I am definitely lost. I tried calling Sean again. Still no answer. Slightly frustrated, I looked up the number for Clear Water Lodge. The receptionist answered, and informed me that I had come in the back way to the lodge. She directed me around the circular drive, and up what looked like a sidewalk. She said it was actually a road to the other side of the campgrounds. Nervous that someone would walk out in front of me, I slowly steered my bike the way she told me to go. Sure enough, the paved road gave way to a gravel path, and led me to another circular drive in front of the main lodge. Off of the roundabout, there was a road leading to a parking lot, and two other roads leading towards more cabins. I parked in front of the main lodge, and walked in through the sliding doors. Just on the other side of the door was Sean.

Chapter 6:   Sean

"Stephen, my man! You made it!" I greeted my friend, Stephen Jones, as he entered the meeting room. He and I have been friends for seven years. We met while working out at the gym in college. We were both heading towards the same machine at the same time. To keep from having to wait around a long while, we worked in our sets together. During our workout, I learned we were both from St. Louis. We asked each other which high school each attended. It turns out that we went to rival schools. So, every now and then, we let that spur our competition. As the saying goes, the rest was history. Stephen was even one of my groomsman in my wedding.

Giving me a handshake and a one armed hug, Stephen said, "Yeah, I made it. What's up with your phone? I have been calling you."

"Man, I apologize! I just learned that the reception out here is practically non-existent. I have not been able to call out myself. I'm glad you were able to find your way ok."

"Relatively, but I'm here now. Hey, thanks for bringing my bags here for me. You saved me a trip home." Stephen had been at work this morning for a few hours, and was not going to be off in time to make it to Doc's office to ride the chartered bus down. Instead, he chose to ride his motorcycle down and meet us here. "Dawg, I did not feel comfortable riding through Potosi, but I'm here." He looked around the room, and said, "Have I missed much?"

"No", I answered. "We are getting ready for the first activity since we've arrived. After I was given the keys to our lodging, I took our bags to our room. We are sharing a cabin with two other guys, but I have not seen them yet because they did not ride the bus down here."

"Ah, ok. I'm thirsty. I need something to drink." Stephen said.

"It's over here." I said, guiding Stephen over to my left. There was a small cafeteria off of the lobby in the main lodge. As we walked towards the refreshment table, I noticed Stephen looking around like he was taking inventory of everyone there.

I looked around the room to locate my wife of three years, who I absolutely love being married to. We met at Doc's office. One day, she was walking out of the office as I was going in. Being the gentleman I am, I stepped back, and held the door open for her to walk through. She said, 'hello'. Then, she smiled so sweetly, and thanked me for holding the door. Her beautiful eyes were so captivating that she had me at 'hello'.

Finally, my eyes found Lisa in the room. She was sitting near the front of the room with her back to me. Next to her were three other ladies, seeming to enjoy the conversation they were having. I pointed, and said to Stephen, "There she is. Lisa is over there with those women. Do you want to go speak to her?" I said as I began leading the way, but before Stephen could answer my question, I saw Doc out of the corner of my eye. She was nearby greeting others. I wanted to make sure Stephen met her.

"Hey!" I grabbed Stephen's arm. "Before we go over to Lisa, I want you to meet Doc."

"Okay", he answered, and shrugged. We walked over to Doc and waited until she had finished speaking to two women. Before she could greet me, I greeted her.

"Doc!" I waved to her. She smiled when she recognized me.

"Hello, Sean! How wonderful it is that you made it?!" she said after a brief hug. "Where is Ms. Lisa?"

I pointed over my shoulder, and said. "She is sitting over there. We were getting ready to join her, but I wanted to speak to you first. May I introduce you to my friend Stephen?" Not waiting for her answer, I turned to Stephen, "Doc, meet Stephen. Stephen, meet Doc."

Doc stretched out her right hand, and Stephen accepted it. "Hello, Stephen. Welcome to the retreat."

"Hello! It is nice to meet you, and thanks for the welcome." Stephen said, and smiled.

"Have you ever been to a chiropractor?" She asked.

"No, but I don't think I need to see one at this time. I am currently seeing a physical therapist for my pain", he replied.

"Hmm. I see. Humor yourself. Why don't you grab one of those questionnaires. If you answer no to every single question, then you, sir, definitely do not need a chiropractor." She paused. "When you have figured out when you need to get chiropractic care, I hope you will consider letting us take care of you at Dynamic Chiropractic." Doc smiled so sweetly and walked away.

"Sure thing," Stephen responded. Turning to me, "Why do I feel like she just challenged me?"

I chuckled. Stephen is so competitive, it's funny sometimes. I did not want to egg him, but she had just challenge him. She had done me the same way when I spoke to her at a health fair. She had handed me the paper a piece of paper to let me determine that I, in fact, needed to be adjusted.

I led Stephen over to the questionnaires. He picked it up and began to read aloud.

"Do I have constant muscle tightness that is never really relieved for long? Um, yes; but who doesn't? It is due to stress." Stephen said.

I laughed. Stephen looked at me confused, and asked, "What is so funny?"

I slapped my hand on his shoulder, and said, "My man. I hate to be the bearer of bad news, but you just lost the challenge with Doc. You didn't even make it past the first question without saying 'yes'. You need to get to the chiropractor." I answered.

Stephen was silent for a few moments while he processed what had happened. Then, he looked back at the list and read several more of the questions. *Do I have numbness and tingling in my arms, hands, legs, or feet? Does it hurt to move? Have I fallen or been in an accident? Does my back pain prevent me from doing what I like to do? Do I have regularly occurring headaches or migraines?*

"Well, here is one question I can definitely say no to, *Do I have irregular periods and/or painful cramps?*" Stephen said.

I chuckled and shook my head at him.

"Also, why didn't you tell me you had a fine ass doctor for your chiropractor? I wouldn't mind letting her take care of me." He said.

"First of all, I don't trip off of her looks." Stephen gave me this look that said, *'Who do you think you are talking to?* "Maybe when I first became a patient, I paid it some attention. However, NOW I don't trip off of it. Is that better?" I said. He nodded, and muttered 'That's what I thought' under his breath

Then, a little louder, he said, "Take me to Lisa so I can hug my sis."

Chapter 7:   Nina

"Hmmmm. I would love to have his hands on me," Kelly said while leaning into my shoulder. "He is one beautiful specimen."

My name is Nina Scott. Kelly and I have been friends since the first grade. I had convinced her to attend this weekend's retreat with me. She has never been to a chiropractor and knows very little about chiropractic. I do my best to teach her the benefits of getting adjusted, but I am not as good at communicating it as Doc. So, this weekend presented the best opportunity for Kelly to learn about it in a fun, informal setting.

With or without Kelly, I had planned to be here. This was my third retreat. I came last year, and loved it. Honestly, I just love going on retreats. They give me a much needed change of pace, and allow me to recharge and re-focus. Clear Water Lodge would be no different. I think we all lose cell phone reception when we drive through the gate onto the campgrounds.

This year's theme is Creating Your Inner Peace: How to De-stress Your Life, if I recall correctly. Throughout the weekend we will be meditating, exercising, doing cooking classes, and more. I even saw painting with a twist on there. That is a big trend back home. Right now, we are kicking off the weekend at the Meet and Greet/Welcome; and Kelly is trying to meet this guy, who has caught her eye. I personally do not know him, but a few moments ago, I overheard someone say "Stephen", to which he responded.

"Do you know him?" Kelly asked, and nodded in his direction.

"Not really. I overheard someone call him Stephen a few moments ago," I replied.

"Well, I hope to get to know him throughout the weekend," Kelly said. "Let's go check out the refreshments. I'm getting hungry."

Kelly and I walked over to the long table that had an array of fruits, cheeses, meats, and crackers. Recently, having overhauled and changed my eating habits, I bypassed a lot of it. I eat very little sugar. I avoid foods that have a lot of sugar in it, naturally and/or artificially. Therefore, I did not eat the cantaloupe, watermelon, honeydew melon, banana, or grapes. Thankfully, there were fruit available I can eat, such as apples, oranges, strawberries, blueberries, and black berries. I did not touch the cheese, crackers, or the meat. My beverage was water.

Kelly, however, still partakes in some of these foods. She had her plate filled with cantaloupe, cheddar cheese, slices of beef summer sausage, and hard salami. Her beverage of choice was tea with several packets of sugar.

As she dumped packets of sugar into her tea, I looked at her and said, "You do not need to eat all of that sugar."

Kelly looked up at me, looked down at her plate, and then back at me. "I don't have much sugar here. What are you talking about?"

Just as I was getting ready to address the sugar content on her plate, Doc approached us. She had been walking around the room greeting everyone, when she finally made her over to this side of the room.

"Hello, Nina! It is so wonderful of you to join us for the weekend," Doc said as she leaned in to hug me. I absolutely love my doctor to pieces. She is sweet, loving, down-to-earth, and very personable. Although she is such a sweet person, she is also very straightforward. She does not beat around the bush when speaking. As we released each other, she said, "Please, introduce me to your guest."

I turned to Kelly, and said, "Doc, meet Kelly. We've been friends for a very long time. She has heard so much about your office and is considering becoming a patient. She has never been to a chiropractor. Since we were allowed to bring a guest to the retreat, she was, naturally, my first choice."

Turning to face Kelly, Doc extended her right hand, and said, "Hello, Kelly. It is a pleasure to meet you. We have planned an amazing weekend. I hope you will learn a great deal and enjoy yourself. If you have any questions throughout the course of the weekend that Nina is not able to answer, please do not hesitate to ask."

"Thank you! I will keep that in mind," Kelly replied. After Doc left to greet other guests, Kelly turned to me, and said sarcastically, "I'm considering becoming a patient, huh?"

I shrugged, and said, "Yeah. You just didn't know it; but now you do", I said. "I am telling you. By the end of this weekend, you will be committed to becoming a patient. You just wait and see."

"Oh, we'll see", Kelly said sarcastically, and turned her attention back to her plate.

I shrugged again and turned my attention back to the other people in the room. I was looking for my soror, Sharon. I saw her heading to receive her room assignment earlier, but was not able to speak to her. When we found out that we were both attending the retreat, we had agreed to get together. She also said her husband might come along on the trip. At the time of our conversation, she did not yet know if he would attend; but shared her plans to work on convincing him to come.

Spotting Sharon, I got Kelly's attention "Hey, I see someone I work with. I want you to meet her. She is the one who told me about Doc." I directed Kelly over to Sharon Lyle. "She is also one of my sorority sisters."

Sharon and I are both instructors at the community college. She is in the Biology department while I am in the Chemistry department. We met a couple of years ago in the parking lot of the campus. Several times, on different occasions, I had noticed a car parked in the faculty lot with the license plate frame that read Sigma Rho Rho, and wondered who my soror might be. Weeks would go by before I would ever happen to be in the parking lot at the same time as her. When I finally did see her, it had been one day after having a rough day at work. Yet, seeing Sharon brought me joy! We became good friends after that day.

"Sharon! How are you?" I greeted her and gave her a hug. "Well, don't you look Rhoyal in your blue?"

"You know I repRHOsent every chance I get. How are you? And, by the way, you are looking fabulous yourself. I can tell you are still in the gym. Those weights are slimming you down quite a bit," she said.

"Thanks!" I smiled. I have been in the gym for over six months. However, I had not noticed any of the changes. I could feel the difference, but did not see it as easily as others. I think it is partly due to the fact that I do not have a full length mirror in my house. So, I only see my body in sections. My clothes are fitting loosely. Therefore, I know my body is changing.

Not wanting to focus on me any longer, I changed the topic of conversation by introducing Kelly to Sharon. Turning towards Kelly, I said, "Sharon, meet my friend, Kelly."

Sharon and Kelly shook hands and exchanged greetings. Ten minutes into the evening, and you could not tell Kelly and Sharon had just met. The three of us eventually made our way to the other side of the room where the chairs were set up for an icebreaker and other activities. There were three seats open next to a lady named Lisa Struthers. We asked her if anyone was sitting next to her. She said not to her right, but she was holding the two seats to her left for her husband and their friend. We thanked her, and sat down next to her.

When Sharon realized it was Lisa I had been speaking to, Sharon greeted her, and then introduced her to us as her suite mate. Shortly thereafter, our trio grew to a quartet.

Chapter 8:   Lisa

My name is Lisa Struthers; Sean's wife. I am super excited about participating in this year's annual retreat because this is my first retreat with my husband. I do not know why, but I feel like this weekend will be life changing. This is the first weekend getaway we have had this year. I have been so busy with my personal training company, teaching classes, certifying trainers, as well as managing private clients. In the past twelve months, the demand for my services has more than doubled.

I have been at this Meet and Greet for fifteen minutes now, and I still have not seen my husband. I have not seen him since everyone was assigned their lodging. I would text him, but I left my phone in the room by accident.

Sharon, my suite mate, and I had been so heavy in a conversation while leaving the room that I did not notice I was phoneless. Although my room was in this building, I was not going to walk all the way back to my room to get it. I was going to have to see him when he got here. He was probably waiting on Stephen to arrive.

Not long after Sharon and I had arrived at the Meet and Greet, I told her I would meet up with her before the Meet and Greet was over, and excused myself to the ladies' room. Since learning I was pregnant, I always have to pee. While I was in the stall, my thoughts went back to earlier this evening when Sharon and I first checked into our suite. I was not able to shake the feeling that she seemed familiar. I do not recall ever meeting her. Yet, and still, she seems very familiar. Her eyes felt like I've looked into them before. The more I spoke to her, the stronger the feeling became. I don't know.

I washed my hands and dried them. At the same time I reached for the door handle with the paper towel in my hand, the door swung open. A beautiful, older, black woman, who was on crutches, was pushing the door open with her backside. Of course, she did not see me behind her.

"I'm behind you." I said gently, not wanting to startle her.

She looked over her shoulder, and smiled. "Sorry about that." She had the sweetest voice.

Shrugging, I said, "it's okay." I held the door open for her, so we could pass by each other. I wanted to get out of that tiny bathroom as quickly as possible, because someone was in one of the other stalls stinking it up. I needed some fresh air.

When the door closed behind me, I headed through lobby to the main entrance. I was going to step outside briefly, and then return to the Meet and Greet. Perhaps, by then my husband will have made it.

As I walked through the lobby, I saw a nice looking man walking in with his carry-on bag in his left hand and dress bag in his right. He was very well groomed. He had a thin goatee, which was a stark contrast to his thick, ebony eyebrows on his brown skin. Standing more than five feet away, even I could see his beautiful green eyes. He wore a white, collared, button down shirt, with cuff links. His gray slacks were creased so sharply you could cut yourself on them. His dress shoes were black Camuto's. Expensive taste. I wonder what brought him here. He was a bit overdressed for a retreat in the woods.

I approached him slowly, and asked, "Hello. Are you here for the chiropractic retreat?"

Realizing I was talking to him, he stopped and looked at me. Although I knew it was only my imagination, I felt like his eyes were peering right through me. I felt naked. "Yes, I am. Maybe you can direct me to Doc or her assistant? I was told I could pick up my lodging assignment from one of them." Extending his hand to me, he said, "By the way, my name is Marcus. What is yours?" he said in a very deep voice.

"I'm Lisa. Nice to meet you. I would shake your hand, but your hands are full." I smiled. He returned the smile; and what a sexy smile he had. Hey! I am married; not blind. Pointing towards the cafeteria off of the lobby, I told him, "If you follow this walkway all the way around to the back of the room, you will find the assistant at the entrance to the patio. You can't miss him. He is sitting at a table by the door."

Marcus flashed me another smile, nodded his head, and said "Thanks" as he headed off in the direction I showed him. Once he had passed me, I stole a glance over my shoulder. Nice body! I hurried on out the front door into the cool night. The lobby had become quite warm.

When the cool air hit me, it reminded me I was not dressed for the weather. My shirt was too thin to protect me from the falling temps. I shivered slightly. I crossed my arms in front of me and rubbed my hands up and down my arms to warm them. The ladybugs were less aggressive than they had been over an hour ago. Ahead of me, I could see a male figure approaching. It was my husband.

"Hey, Daddy!" I said. Hearing my voice, he did a light jog until he was right in front of me.

Wrapping his arms around me, and planting his face in the crook of my neck, he inhaled in my scent. Then, he exhaled and whispered, "Hey, Mommy." He kissed me softly on my ear. "What are you doing out here in the cold?" He pulled apart from me and looked over his shoulder. He smiled slyly, "Your nipples are hard."

I playfully swatted at him. "I was getting a quick breath of fresh air. Have you heard from Stephen? I have not seen him yet," I said.

"No. I have not spoken to him since this morning. I'm having trouble getting reception, and haven't been able to call out. I hope he finds it ok." Turning me towards the lodge, he directed me back inside. "Let's get out of this cool air. I don't want you to get sick." He wrapped his arm around my shoulders and led the way. I love being in his arms because I fit perfectly.

As we walked through the sliding door entrance of the lodge, the receptionist looked up from the computer screen and smiled at us briefly. We returned the smile and continued past the desk and into the cafeteria.

Inside the room, I kissed Sean on the lips, and told him I will go find three seats for us while he went back to lobby to wait for

Stephen. I walked across the room. The chairs were arranged in a large circle. Upon approaching the circle, I saw the older lady I had almost knocked over in the restroom. She was now looking down at her cellphone. I spoke to her again.

"Hello, again." I said. "I apologize for colliding into you at the bathroom earlier."

She looked up. She smiled politely, and responded, "Oh, that's quite alright. You did not hurt me." She reached out her hand to me, "My name is Jennifer. What is your name?"

"My name is Lisa. Nice to meet you." I sat in the row in front of her. I wanted to make sure I had seats saved for Sean and Stephen. I, then, turned around to talk to her.

"Is this your first retreat, Ms. Jennifer?" I asked.

"Oh, honey, please do not call me Ms. Jennifer. Jennifer is just fine. And, no. This is not my first retreat. It is my first retreat in a couple of years though. How about you?"

"No. This is not my first time attending, but it is my first time attending it with my husband, Sean. Like myself, he is a patient of Doc," I answered. Then, I asked, "Since this isn't your first retreat, I take it you are a patient of Doc?"

"Yes, I am. I have been her patient since she was in chiropractic school. I just followed her into her practice. I have been a chiropractic patient for many, many years; probably as long as you've been alive. How long have you been married", she said.

"Sean and I have been married for three years, but we still act like newlyweds." I said. "Are you married?"

"Oh, no! I'm not married. However, I do have a man with whom I've been for three years. He is the love of my life." she said.

"The love of your life and you are not married? Why is that," I asked. Inquiring minds wanted to know.

She said, "I'm not interested in being married. That's all." I'm sure there is more to that, but I didn't feel comfortable enough to push the issue. Maybe later on in our friendship I will circle back to that question.

"Did he come with you?" I asked.

"No, he didn't. I decided to come on my own, to give us a little break from one another. It gives us an opportunity to miss each other. In other words, I needed a break from him. He also had another event to attend," she laughed.

Do you have any children?" I asked next.

"You sure are asking a lot of questions. In any other situation, I would have told you 'none of your business; but I won't this time. None that I have birthed myself." At that moment, her phone rang. She looked down at the face of the phone. "I must take this call. Excuse me", she said. She stood with the crutches and moved quickly away.

I turned around and face forward. I decided this was a great place Stephen, Sean and me to sit. Not even moments later, a young lady with two other women behind her approached me. She wanted to know if the seats beside me were occupied. I told her the seats on my right were open, and all three sat down. One of them was my suitemate, Sharon.

Recognizing me, she spoke first, "Hi, Lisa!" She pointed to each of the women with her. "This is my sorority sister, Nina, and her friend, Kelly. Ladies, this is my suitemate, Lisa." We each exchanged greetings.

While continuing their conversation, they were began to include me. I mostly listened. Enjoying their light banter, I thought to myself, I like them. I am going to enjoy hanging with these ladies. They are hilarious. Who knows? I may have just made some new lifelong friends. Just then, I saw movement out of the corner of my eye. Looking to see what it was, I was pleased to see my hubby and our friend, Stephen, approaching.

"Excuse me. Ladies, allow me to introduce you to my husband and our friend." Once they were upon us, I said, "This is Stephen." who reached out and hugged me. When he moved to the side, I wrapped my arms around my husband, kissed him lightly on the lips, and said, "And this one right here is my husband, Sean." I am pretty sure at that moment, I probably looked like a school girl. I still smile super big whenever he comes around me.

Simultaneously, the guys and the ladies all said, "Hello." Then, each lady took turns introducing herself.

"I'm Nina."

"Kelly."

"And, I am Sharon."

"Nice to meet you all," Stephen said and leaned in to shake hands with each person. I noticed he purposely skipped over Kelly to greet her last. I also noticed he held her hand and gaze slightly longer than the other women. "So, are all of you patients of Doc?" he asked.

Kelly pointed at Sharon and Nina and answered, "These two are; but, I'm not. I'm Nina's guest."

"And, I'm Sean's guest," he said. With the once over Stephen gave Kelly, everyone could tell Stephen liked Kelly; and with the bashful look Kelly gave, she had noticed, too. You know what? They *would* make a handsome couple.

At that moment, Doc stepped to the mic. "Good evening, everyone! Thank you for coming out to Dynamic Health Wellness Center's annual weekend chiropractic retreat. We are in for a great time! Are you all ready to have a great time?!" The room of about forty to fifty people quickly filled with the sound of everyone saying variations of 'yes' in response to Doc. "Allow me to introduce myself to those who are guests of our established patients. I'm the owner and physician of Dynamic Health and Wellness Center. We are celebrating eight years of service to the St. Louis area. The theme for this weekend is Creating Your Inner Peace: How to De-stress Your Life. We will teach you how to meditate, make better dietary choices, and much more. By show of hands, how many guests of patients do we have with us this weekend?" Almost half of the room were guests. Doc continued, "Wonderful! Please keep your hands up. Only put your hand down if you have been to a chiropractor before." Five hands went down. More than ten people still had their hands up. Everyone looked around to see whose hands were still up. "Wow! You all may now put your hands down."

"Everyone in this room has experienced stress of some kind at some point. Therefore, I don't have to teach anyone what is 'stress' in that manner. However, did you now that stress falls into three categories? They are brain, body, and chemistry. If you are not surrounding yourself around positive people, places, and things, then you are depositing negativity into your brain, which in turn, becomes a stress on the body. To de-stress your brain, you have to be mindful and conscious of the images to which you expose yourself, the thoughts you allow yourself to have, the words your speak, and the company you keep. Stress on the body is more physical. To de-stress your body, you have to manage your weight, be aware of your posture, and of course get chiropractic adjustments. Yes, that was a plug." The room erupted in laughter. "Lastly, the chemistry. What is 'chemistry'? When I use the word chemistry, I am talking about what you put into your body. To de-stress via chemistry, you have to be mindful of what you put into your mouth. You are overall less stressed when you are eating healthy. You feel a whole lot better when you have eaten a healthy meal of protein, carbs, and the right fats versus how you feel after having eaten fried greasy foods loaded with bad fats. This is not the last time you will hear me say brain, body, chemistry this weekend. It will show up repeatedly throughout the activities we have planned for you."

Doc switched gears and said, "Parents, have you ever given your child advice, only for him or her to ignore it because it came from you? Yet they eagerly took the same advice from someone else? This is the very reason I am not going to stand here and tell our guests how great chiropractic is. Instead, I will let you listen to what other patients have to say. Do we have anyone who is willing to share how they became a patient?"

After a few stories were shared, my husband decided to share his coming to chiropractic moment.

"Hi, Sean", Doc said when he stood up. "What is your story?"

"Hello, everyone. My name is Sean Struthers. I became a patient a few years ago because I was having low back pain, hip discomfort, and headaches. The pain had been going down my leg, along with numbness and tingling. I had injured myself while lifting weights at the gym. At first, I didn't think my pain was anything major. So, I tried self-care. I even continued lifting weights, thinking I was helping my healing process by lifting lighter weights. I used a heating pad, took Ibuprofen, and long hot showers. The pain worsened. One day I saw one of Doc's cards at the gym and gave her a call. I am so glad I did. She got me out of pain. Although most men aren't willing to admit it, I was scared of Doc at first, because I had never been to a chiropractor or knew of anyone who had. However, Doc eased my fears and the rest was history." He returned to his seat.

Doc said, "Thank you, Sean." Then, continued on to the next patient.

I side eyed my husband, and said, "So, you gone just lie like that?" Naturally, he gave me the look that said, "What did I say wrong?" I rolled my eyes and returned my attention back to Doc.

The Meet and Greet led straight into dinner, during which Doc introduced all of the speakers and gave details of what was to come this weekend. Dinner was being held in the dining hall. So, I walked down to the hall with the ladies while Stephen and my husband trailed us. They were speaking in low tones about something. Being nosy, I tried to ear hustle, but I kept getting distracted by what the ladies were saying.

"I heard about that cream!" Sharon exclaimed. "I also heard Doc dispenses it from her office."

"Come again?" I asked. "What kind of cream are you talking about?"

Sharon answered, "I have a girlfriend who says her husband was different after his vasectomy. He was short tempered at times, less patient with people, depressed, and experienced some changes with his sexual performance. She didn't go into details, for which I am glad. She said somehow this topic came up with Doc. She does not know how, but it did. He was instructed to rub this cream on his scrotum twice a day. She said, after about a week, she could see the difference in her husband. He was back to his pre-V self for the most part. He was laidback again."

I laughed. "It sounds so funny to hear you say 'scrotum' like we are in an anatomy class. It's called balls. He was told to rub the cream on his balls." We all laughed.

"So what happened with the sexual changes?" I asked.

"She said her husband's sex drive has been off the chain. She feels like she has a younger husband. He can't keep his hands off of her. She sometimes feel like she has to sleep with one eye open." Sharon finished, still laughing.

We all continued laughing as we passed through the doorway into the dining hall. The dining hall had long tables with chairs on each side. There were twenty tables; ten in the front half of the room, and ten in the back half. Tonight's dinner was being catered by a company that served all organic food that was grown on their farm. It was called farm to table fare. There was going to be a lot of vegetarian options for our usual non-vegetarian dishes.

Nina was ahead of the group. So, she chose a table in the middle of the front ten tables for us all to sit together. Kelly sat to the left of Nina, who sat at the end of the table. Next to Kelly sat Stephen. Across the table from Stephen sat my husband. I sat to his left. Next to me was Sharon.

As we became settled, I saw Jennifer walk in and look around for a table to join. I waited until I had made eye contact before waving her over. "I'll be back", I said to my husband. I got up to meet her half way. Once I was in front of her, I invited her to sit with us. "Jennifer, we have plenty of room at our table. Would you like to sit with us?"

She smiled, "Remind me. Please? What's your name again?" she said.

"It's Lisa." I answered. "I didn't know if you had anyone to sit with, and I didn't want you to sit alone. If not, you may join us."

"Thanks for the invite. I was actually going to sit over here for dinner because I saw someone I know from the gym. Maybe I can catch up with you next time", she said.

"Oh. No problem. Enjoy your dinner! I will see you around", I said. Then, I returned to the table. The appetizers were being served.

"Sharon", Sean said sticking a fork full of food in his mouth. "Where is Anthony? I thought he was coming to the retreat?"

Sharon looked up from the plate she had just pushed away from her. After tasting the unnamable appetizer, she decided it was not very appetizing. "He is going to join us tomorrow. He is out of town for work. He should be landing in about an hour. Thanks for asking about him."

"No problem. I was just thinking about how much I had to sell him on attending the retreat. Since I didn't see him, I figured I must not have done too good of a job", Sean said.

"Know how much I wanted to come, he knew he knew he would not have heard the last of it if he had not come with me", Sharon said. Everyone at the table and understood and laughed.

Then, Sean said, "Happy wife, happy life."

After dinner, I saw Kelly, Sharon, and Nina heading towards the lake and decided to catch up with them since Sean took Stephen to their cabin to show him where they were staying. Stephen wanted to change his clothes.

"Hey ladies! Wait up, please", I called after them. They stopped, and all turned to watch and wait for me to catch up to them. They had not made it too far from the lodge. So, I did not have to jog far.

"Hey, Lisa! Did you enjoy that dinner?" asked Nina.

"It wasn't too bad of a meal. It was just...different. How about y'all?" I replied.

They each answered.

"I could have gone for a pizza instead", answered Sharon.

"Pizza *would* have been better, but dinner was not horrible. I'll say it was an acquired taste", said Nina.

"I couldn't have fed that meal to my dog", said Kelly. "Hopefully, tomorrow will be better."

We continued walking towards the lake. Under foot, the path changed from paved to gravel. We could hear the rocks crunch and roll as we passed over them. Overhead, the night sky was sprinkled with stars. As our distance increased from the lodge, our shadows no longer came from the iridescent lights from within the lodging, but from the occasional light poles. We could hear all sorts of night animals. I can only name two of the night sounds; an owl and a bat.

Only a few feet from the lake's shore, I broke the silence.

"There are a few breakout sessions this evening. The one I'm looking forward to is the slow core movement class, which is also at the same time as painting with a twist. I think it's called sensual yoga. According to the description, we will be doing various yoga poses while getting in touch with our sensuality. I've never heard of yoga in that sense. I'm curious as to how this works. The itinerary for tomorrow sounds even more exciting. I'm looking forward to hearing the Sex Therapist speak. I can't wait to hear how sex and inner peace go hand and hand", I said

"You?!" exclaimed Kelly, and we all laughed.

"Personally, I *can* think of some ways sex can help with inner peace. And, honey, some good sex can make you sleep like a baby." said Nina.

"I agree," said Sharon, "especially when everything goes right. When it's good, it is good. When it's bad, it can mess up your whole night."

Laughing, I said, "Ain't that the truth! That's how my husband really ended up at Doc's office."

"Wait a minute," Nina said, "He said he had hurt his back at the gym."

"He lied. Hold up, let me back that up. I shouldn't say that," I paused to gather my thoughts. "Maybe he did hurt his back at the gym, but that is not how he initially hurt his back. Let me tell you how he really hurt his back."

"If I had to title this story, I would call it...Slippery when wet." We all burst into laughter. "Sean is much older than me. At the time, we had been married for about a year. Despite what people may think, he does not have trouble in the sex department. People think that because he is closer to   fifty, he must have erectile dysfunction. Thankfully, that has not been a problem for him. In fact, at that time, his sex drive seemed to be increasing since he was going to the gym. That man could not keep his hands off of me.

"One night, while I was in the shower, he decided to join me. No problem. What a great way to destress after the day I'd had. We bathed each other, and played with each other. He planted a kiss on my lips, and I reached up to wrap my arms around his neck. While he's bending to pick me up, my heart starts racing because I was so excited! I'm a petite woman, as you can tell, and he is every bit of six feet tall. Besides, I love being picked up. Anyway, it had been a long time since he had swept me off my feet like that. Having returned to working out regularly made him feel like Superman.

"Well, Sean picked me up in that shower! Baby, I closed my eyes, and let my head fall back; anticipating the next body shaking sensation. That next moment, I did feel that body shaking sensation. Yeah, all one hundred fifty three of my pounds, five foot nothing frame hitting the shower floor, and landing on my ass. HARD! I will NEVER EVER forget the sound of my bare wet skin and the weight of my body hitting that floor.

"When I looked up from the floor at Sean, all I saw was his panic stricken face as it was coming towards me very quickly. All I kept thinking was: "Shit! I can't move! His big ass is getting ready to fall on me."

I continued my story as the ladies struggled to catch their breath from laughing, "After he finally got himself to his feet, he bent down to pick me up. In doing so, he caught a cramp. It caught him off guard and off balance, causing him to lose his footing on the slippery floor, as well as, lose his grip on my wet body at the same time. He couldn't stop what was getting ready to happen." The ladies were doubled over in laughter. In between breaths, Kelly screams and gasped for air.

"Let me just say this, I could not sit for a week! What kind of job do I have?! A desk job. Perfect! The pain progressed. I had pain going down my leg and my foot had started going numb. I told Sean to stick to lifting weights and leave my ass alone."

By now, we were all laughing with tears running down our face. Sharon laughed the hardest, though. She admitted to us how that story reminded her of her sexiness gone wrong.

"Speaking of falls," Sharon said, "I have a story for you. I came to Doc five years ago because I was trying to be sexy. But, before I tell you, we need to be heading to the lodge for Painting with a Twist. Or are we going to the yoga class?"

"Let's go to the painting with a twist, because we can talk while we paint. We can't talk during yoga. It's all about breathing."

Chapter 9:   Sharon

Lisa checked her watch for the time. She pressed a button that lit up the face of the watch a bright blue. "We have less than ten minutes to get there." She agreed.

"Well", I began, "While we walk, I'll talk. If I had to title my story, I would call it 'Dance for Me'. I went to Doc's office complaining of knee and ankle pain. My knee and ankle had been killing me for weeks! One of my cousins had suggested I go see her. So, I did.

Around two months prior to my first visit, one of my younger cousins celebrated her 23rd birthday. She wanted to do something *different*; and so she did.

My cousin, Elisa, invited some girlfriends and family members out to join her at a place called The Dollhouse. We received an hour of instruction that included a sexy chair dance and ended with pole dancing.

Before we started, we were allowed to pick our props, such as hats and boas. Then, we were taught a simple, but oh so sexy routine to Bey's *Partition*. I really enjoyed learning this dance. I thought it would be terrible of me to not give an encore performance for Brian. I promised myself, he was going to get a show he will soon never forget. I sat on the couch and waited for him in my peekaboo black leotard over a pair of sheer pantyhose with the seam up the back of the leg and my red bottom shoes on."

Nina interrupted, "Girl! Were you rocking your Louboutin's?"

"Um, no, I was just wearing some shoes with red bottoms. Anyway, just after Brian walked in, I led him to the couch where he was to watch me dance for him. Using the remote control, I pushed play on the stereo and dimmed the lights. When the beat dropped, I walked over to the chair. Slowly, and as seductively as I could, I slid my hands down the sides of the chair and sat into a wide legged squat. The same as I had gone down, I came back up. Sexily, I walked around to the left side of the chair. Never taking my eyes off of Brian, I picked up my left leg to place my left foot in the seat of the chair, and lean forward to caress my leg.

However, I completely missed the seat of the chair. Instead, it landed on the rung of the chair between the chair legs. Because I was leaning forward to rub my leg, my weight pushed the chair away from me, and across the freshly waxed hardwood floor; sending me into a split." I stopped walking, and faced them with my hands up and palms facing them, "Did I mention I've never been able to do a split before?"

Nina, Kelly, and Lisa hollered and doubled over with laughter. They could not take another step. In between breaths, Kelly said, "Way to remix the dance and make it your own."

Laughingly and sarcastically I said, "Right." Then, I continued, "Anyway, wanting to forget that just happened, I did all that I could to suppress that memory so much so that I had succeeded. In fact, I did everything short of breaking up with Brian. When I saw Doc and she asked me if I had fallen, I did not think twice about saying 'No'. Girl! Why did Doc give me this look like, "Stop lying?" It was if she had been there when it had happened. Well, I may be exaggerating a little or maybe slightly paranoid. Whatever." I said.

I paused to catch my breath, then continued, "During the whole visit I felt like she was looking right through my body, because of the questions she asked me while examining me. Doc asked me, "Have you noticed a change in your cycle?" That question had caught me off guard, but I answered, "Yes and told her I had not had a cycle in two months. I had been checking to see if I was pregnant, but the tests kept coming back negative. My OB/GYN also said I was not pregnant and that it was probably due to stress. Then, Doc asked me had I been having the urge to pee frequently? At that time, I did. I could not go far from a bathroom.

"Wait, wait, wait", Kelly interrupted. "Are you telling me all of that happened because you fell? I am confused. You slipped, fell, and bust your ass. As a result, you have a messed up ankle, knee, hips, and low back. Right?"

I looked at Kelly, and answered, "Yes." We were almost at the entrance of the lodge. That was a lot quicker than I had anticipated. We still had more than five minutes left before painting. I had been ahead of the group as we walked. I stopped before the steps and turned to Kelly, "Some of those things I had been experiencing off and on prior to the fall; but after that fall, they became worst. I had even acquired some new symptoms. What is so interesting about it all, is that I did not even realize my symptoms correlated with the achy areas of my body. Doc was so thorough in her exam that she also uncovered that I was gassy, constipated, bloated, short of breath, and having headaches."

Having made it to the top of the steps, I opened the door and help it open for the ladies to walk through.

We walked down the hallway to the stairwell, which we descended to the lower level. People were in line to enter the room. Everyone must have returned at the same time. Ahead of us, I could see Sean and Stephen. Sean looked behind him and spotted Lisa. Smiling, he waved and blew a kiss.

Despite how long the line was, it was moving right along. There were still groups of seats available for me and the ladies to sit together. Nina had made her way ahead of the group. So, we followed her to a group of seats near the front corner of the room. As we selected our easel, Kelly chose the one closest to me.

"So getting chiropractic care fixed all of those problems?" Kelly asked.

"It did for me. Getting adjusted gave me life, child!" I answered. "I saw Doc regularly for two months. After each visit, I could actually feel my body getting better. My pain went away and I was able to walk normally again. At the end of the two months, I could definitely tell I was much healthier. I was sleeping better at night, having regular bowel movements, regular menstrual cycles, no longer having gas pains or belching, knee and ankle pain free, and down five pounds. Now, the last benefit was an added bonus. Who knew irregular bowel movements could affect your weight?"

"Oh, really?!" Kelly incredulously asked. She was having a hard time believing what she was hearing.

"Really." I answered. By the look on her face, I could tell she was not sure how to process what she was being told. How could she if she has never experienced anything like it? It is easier to process new information when you have a relatable experience or memory. However, as an African American female, I can understand why she cannot relate. Most of my Black brothers and sisters have not been to a chiropractor. If they have been, it was because they were in an accident. So, they are under the assumption that you only go to a chiropractor when you have been in an accident or have otherwise injured yourself. What can I say? That was me, once upon a time. Having become a patient of Doc's, I now understand the value of receiving regular chiropractic care. I sometimes wonder why anyone would want to live without it.

"So, now you know that what your friends were saying about you is true", Nina said.

"What do you mean?" I asked. Clearly, I was confused. What could she know about what my friends say about me?

"At first, it was just a hunch. Now, I'm certain of it," Nina began, "You are full of shit!"

Their laughter erupted so loudly that a couple of people nearby turned to see what we were laughing about. We dropped our heads down, picked up our paint brushes, and pretended to be painting.

I kept my head down until I thought it was safe for me to look up without being watched. Simultaneously, as I lifted my head, I felt someone standing beside me. I looked over to my left and saw Jennifer standing there. She smiled her greeting.

"Is this seat taken?" she asked and waited patiently for a response.

Lisa answered before I could, "It is now. How nice of you to join us." Lisa reached over to pull the chair out for her, but Jennifer interrupted her.

"Thanks! I got it." Jennifer said. She pulled the chair out, and then laid slid her crutch to the floor beside the legs of her seat. Then, with such smooth movements, she sat down in her chair. We all watched in silence as she positioned herself.

"It's Jennifer, right?" Lisa asked. She can recall names. She can recall faces. However, she struggles to recall whose face goes with whose name. Tonight, she had met quite a few people and was having a more difficult time than usual. Is this baby brain already?

Having settled herself into the chair, Jennifer finally answered, "Yes. Please remind me of your name again."

"My name is Lisa, and these are my friends." Lisa identified each of us. We each nodded our greetings with a smile.

"Nice to meet you all. I'm Jennifer. Just call me Jennifer; not Ms. Jennifer. How are you all doing tonight?" In unison, we all answered 'Good', and deflected the question back to her. "I'm doing pretty well. Thanks for asking. I may be doing even better, since I've joined the liveliest part of the room. When I came in, I could tell the party was over here. So, I decided to join you all."

Nina stopped texting, placed her hands on the table, and tilted her head to the right. "Wait a minute! What I just heard Jennifer say was, she saw some class clowns and wanted to join the circus. I'm trying to figure out how I should feel about this."

Jennifer piped in, "Honored. Let me guess. You are the ring leader."

We all laughed again. I could tell I was going to love being around Jennifer.

Just then, the instructor walked to the front of the room to explain to everyone how our paint session will go and what time this room will be opened in the morning to pick up our artwork. His name was Mr. Irving. When he showed us what we were painting, I rolled my eyes, and said, "Why am I not surprised that we are painting a twisted spine?! If someone had asked me, I would have suggested a chiseled naked man. But, hey, no one asked me."

"Just paint." Nina said.

****

The next morning, everyone was expected to be at the lake for the morning meditation. Lisa was still in the room when I left. She told me she would catch up with me. As I got closer to the lake, I spotted Kelly and Nina; noticing me, they waved me over.

"Good morning, ladies", I greeted. I bent over at the waist and placed my yoga mat to the right of Nina, just as Stephen placed his mat next to the left of Kelly. When did he get here?

"Good morning, ladies", he said in his deep baritone voice. At that moment, his voice sounded way more seductive than they should have. Can you blame me, really? Stephen was breathtakingly gorgeous; well sculpted body, handsome face, and a smile that melts you.

Startled, Kelly snapped her head around to the left to see who had spoken. Obviously, I was not the only one who had not noticed him approaching. When she saw that it was Stephen, she was all smiles. I could not tell which was shining the brightest: the rising sun or her smile. "Good morning", she replied shyly.

"Do you mind if I sit next to you?" he asked Kelly. He gave her a little smile as she blushed and looked away. He was so charming that he had me blushing too.

"Not at all," she answered; keeping her eyes facing forward all the while trying not to blush.

"Good morning, ladies and gentleman. My name is Mares, and I will be leading us in yoga and meditation. Please stand and step to the end of your mat."

Following directions, I walked to the end of my mat. Suddenly, I felt the little hairs on my arm raise. Someone was approaching me. When I looked to my right, I saw that it was my husband, Anthony. He had finally made it to the retreat. He did not ride down here with me on the bus because his flight had not made it back to St. Louis from a Las Vegas. Seeing his face made me very happy. I had been really missing my baby.

"Did you miss me, Mommy", as if he really needed to ask.

I wrapped my arms around his neck. With a hug and kiss, I whispered, "More than you know, Daddy." He held me tighter, pulled me closer, and returned my hug and kiss. Then, I whispered, "I can think of a few other places you can kiss."

"Oooo, you are so nasty; but I love it." Pulling away from me, he said, "I have to take my things to the cabin. Let me get out of here. I will see you at breakfast. I have to take my things to the cabin." He started to walk off, but doubled back to me, and left a trail of kisses on my face; beginning on my forehead and ending on my chin. Then, he left.

I returned my attention back to the meditation and found that everyone had sat down and were listening to the next set of instructions. I tried my best to lose myself in meditation, but I just could not. My concentration left with my husband. These days, all I thought about was making love to my husband. It seems like ever since we found out we were expecting, my hormones have been all over the place, and I am always horny. If these people were not out here, I would have grabbed me a hand full of his... Ha! Let me quit playing. I am too much of a scaredy cat.

"Just take deep...slow...breaths", Mares said, breaking into my dirty thoughts. The harder I tried to focus on my breathing, the more gutter my thoughts became. After what seemed like forever, Mares finally brought the meditation to a close. Yes! I have been ready to go.

Chapter 10: Stephen

I could not wait for the meditation to end. I had to pee something terrible; the story of my life. As I walked out of the men's bathroom, I spotted Sean and Lisa walking into the lodge. One look at them, and anyone could tell what they have been up to. They were glowing. I just hope that if they were in our cabin they cleaned up afterwards.

"I'm so glad you two could join us", I said sarcastically as I approached them.

Sean turned around first, "Whatever. Have you found somewhere to sit yet?" Lisa turned around second, and simply smiled.

"No, I haven't found a table yet. I'm just now getting here myself." I looked away from them and began surveying the room. "Where do you want to sit?" I asked. Sean saw an open table in the back corner of the dining hall.

"Let's sit there", he pointed. Sean led the way while Lisa and I followed him over. Before we made it to the table, Lisa spotted Sharon, Nina, and Kelly walking into the room. So, she waved them over to join us. Nice! Just what I was hoping for; another opportunity to behold Kelly's captivating beauty.

As the ladies made their way over to us, we all greeted them.

Kelly was getting ready to sit at the far end of the table by Nina, but I stopped her. "Kelly. I was hoping you would come sit by me.

I saved this seat just for you." Did she just blush? Ah, yeah! I have definitely gotten her attention. She obliged me, and sat next to me. I smiled my appreciation. Immediately when Kelly stepped beside me, I felt this indescribable energy. I could feel it deep down in my soul. It seemed to draw me nearer to her. I could feel my heart beating faster. It was the same feeling I had noticed when we were at meditation, which, by the way, was much more challenging this morning than any other morning.

Usually, meditation comes easily for me because it is a part of my routine. This morning, however, was not the case. I did not realize meditation would prove to be that difficult while sitting next to Kelly. My intentions for sitting next to her was to rattle her. Instead it was I who could not focus. Sitting next to her and inhaling her scent stirred some things in me, which surprised me. It has been a long while since I have had a solid erection. I have not had one since the accident. In fact, the only time I have been able to successfully achieve one, whether intentional or unintentional, was when I get that morning wood. Just as quickly as I pay the water bill, so goes the sensation evading me until the next morning. How I miss when it would rise on demand.

Honestly, I had given up on thinking I could rise to the occasion. My, now ex-girlfriend, was a model with a bad ass body, but she no longer aroused me. We had been together about a year and a half before my accident. We were so in love with each other. After nine months, we moved into an apartment together. There was no doubt in my mind, I was going to make her my wife. However, my certainty shifted to doubt after the car accident.

The new reality after the accident ended our love euphoria. We were now facing the not so glamorous aspect of our relationship; the part of the relationship that required work. This was not so easy for her. The first few months of taking care of me were fine at first. Then, it became burdensome. The strain took a toll on me physically, mentally, and emotionally, which in turn took a toll on her. As I appeared to be getting better, our relationship continued to head towards disrepair. When she would walk around the house in a negligee or simply butt naked, it did not arouse me. She thought it was because I was cheating; but it wasn't.

Yet, here I was sitting next to, relatively, a stranger and feeling some stirring. When I heard Nina speak, my thoughts returned to the present.

"Hey! Where have you two been?" Nina asked. No sooner had that come out of her mouth did she wish she that it had stayed in her head. One look at them, and she followed up with "Never mind. Your afterglow tells it all." Once again, Lisa simply smiled.

While everyone were still selecting their seats and taking off their jackets, Doc stopped by the table and said, "Please, help yourself to the food when you are ready. You don't have to wait." Then, she was gone.

"Thanks", we called behind her. Doc probably did not hear us because someone walked up to greet her.

I looked down at Kelly. Her head was turned in the direction that Doc had gone. I lightly rested my hand on her right shoulder and said, "Let's eat." Although breakfast was being served, I fantasizing about how Kelly's lips tasted.

His eyes. His smile. His voice. His scent. His energy. Oh my, my, my! They are all so intoxicating; just sensory overload. My heart beats faster the closer I get to him. I noticed it during meditation. Now, he wants me to sit next to him. In my head, I told him no because this attraction I was feeling was growing more and more intense. Instead, I fixed my mouth to say ok and walked right over to him.

After Doc announced that we could serve ourselves, I could feel Stephen looking at me. I did not turn to look at him until I felt his hand on my shoulder. He said, "Let's eat." For some reason, my mind went totally gutter. I felt like he meant more than some pancakes.

When I stood up, he stood, and assisted me with my chair. What a gentleman! I stepped to the side to let him walk ahead of me, but instead, he stretched out his left arm; signaling for me to lead the way. The first couple of steps I took were awkward because I was feeling very self-conscious. I could definitely feel his eyes all over my backside. The distance from our table to the food felt like a country mile.

There were lines on either side of the buffet table. I joined the line on the back side of the table because it was shorter. Stephen followed. The food looked delicious. There was a fruit platter with Blue, Black, and Raspberries, Strawberries, Honey Dew, Cantaloupe, Apples slices, and Orange slices all arranged into the design of a butterfly. Even with pieces of fruit missing, it was still beautiful. Next to the fruit were the Belgian waffles and pancakes that the server had just brought out to the table. You could still see the steam coming off of the pan. Beside these pans were the usual toppings for those who wished to partake in them: cherries, whipped cream, Maple syrup, strawberry syrup, and blueberry syrup.

Further down the table were the meats. There was beef bacon and turkey sausage, and baked cod. At the end of the table, there were a couple of options for the eggs. You could either get scrambled eggs or an omelet cooked to order.

On the refreshment table, there was fresh squeezed orange juice, coffee, almond milk, and water. In a bowl, in the middle of the table, were slices of lemon. Next to the bowl were packets of cream and sugar.

Although I went through the line before Stephen, I chose to wait for him to get his bottle of water so we can walk back to the table together. My wait was very brief.

"Kelly, what is your last name?" Stephen asked while we trekked back to our table.

"Jackson", I answered. "What is your last name?"

"Jones. Do you have a man?" he asked.

"No, I don't. Do you have a girlfriend?" I asked. I wondered if he would be honest or not. Then, again, it really is not only a matter of if he is or is not being honest, but do I believe him.

He answered, "Not at this time. I'm very single. Do you have a girlfriend?"

I stopped in my tracks, and looked at him incredulously. Did he really just ask me if I had a girlfriend? Sensing that I was no longer walking behind him, he stopped and looked back at me.

"What," he said nonchalantly, "You act like it doesn't happen. Just as easily as I can have a girlfriend; so can you." He softly chuckled to himself before turning on his heels, "So? Do you have a girlfriend?"

Still in shock that he would ask me something like that, I did not follow him right away. I rolled my eyes at the back of his head. I could not believe I was getting ready to even entertain that question with an answer. "No, I do NOT have a girlfriend."

"I was just checking. For all I know, you may be into playing for both teams", he laughs again and shrug his shoulders.

We had finally arrived at our table. Lisa and Nina were there getting ready to dig into their food. Stephen sat his food down on the table and quickly, yet smoothly, pulled my seat out before I could sit my food down on the table. I stole a glance across the table at Nina as I slid into my chair and caught her peeping over her fork as she placed a bit of food into her mouth.

"Thank you, Stephen. That is very nice of you." I said.

"The pleasure is definitely all yours... I mean, mine", he said laughingly. "Really! The pleasure is mine."

I laughed. That was kind of funny. "Just full of jokes, huh?" I said.

After helping me scoot my chair up to the table, he took his seat next to me, and began to eat.

We had been silent for a few moments before I said, "So how long have you been with your boyfriend?"

Stephen had been taking a drink from his bottle of water when I hit him with that question. Taken by surprised, he started choking. A little bit of water dribbled down his chin. He reached in front of him for one of the napkins I had brought back to the table, and wiped his mouth. I could not stop laughing.

Swallowing, he answered, "That is one team I do not play for. I love women too much and have no interest in men like that."

I shrugged, "Well, you said you didn't have a girlfriend at this time. That didn't meant you don't have a boyfriend. I'm just saying." Now it was his turn to just look at me. I smiled and winked at him while I returned to eating my breakfast.

From the corner of my eye, I could see him still looking at me with a smile. After I chewed my food, I said, "Take a picture. It will last longer." Then, I grabbed my cup of orange juice with my pinkie out and sipped slowly.

Stephen laughed. In a slow and low tone, he said, "I thought about it, but I wasn't sure how you would feel about someone you barely knew taking your picture."

I blushed.

"So, Stephen, how old are you," I asked.

"I'm 41. How young are you?" he answered while scooping up a fork full of hash browns.

"Nice. That's real nice: 'how young are you?'" I replied.

"Well…" He paused to sip his apple juice, and then continued, "You are young…and very beautiful, I might add."

Again, I blushed. I blushed so hard that my jaw began to ache because I had food in my mouth. It is painful trying to smile in the midst of chewing. Because the pain was slow to dissipate, it made it difficult to swallow my food before speaking. Finally, I was able to say, "36." Once again, from the corner of my eye, I could see him smiling in my direction before continuing to eat.

Down at the other end of the table, I saw Jennifer pulling up a chair. She had a pleasant smile on her face. When you look at her, she seems so innocent. When she opens her mouth, you learn otherwise.

"Who is that," Stephen nodded in Jennifer's direction.

The guys had not met her yet because they were not sitting with us last night when we were painting. So, I told him, "That is Ms. Jennifer."

"Oh," he said. "She looks amazing for her age. Her soft white hair looks great against her chocolate skin. If it wasn't for her hair, I would say she is no more than fifty years old. Her body is so toned! You can tell she has really taken great care of herself through the years." Then, he returned his attention back to me. "Kelly, do you have any children?" Stephen asked.

"No, I do not. Do you have any?" I replied.

"No. Do you want children," he asked next.

"Yes, I do. What about you," I said.

He answered, "I definitely want some one day. I would love to have a few min-ME's running around."

"How many is a few?" I asked.

"Three or four. I love children. How many do you want?" He answered.

"I'm not sure. At least two." At that moment, my cell phone chimed. The sound startled me. This was the first time my phone had rang or buzzed since being here. When I looked down at the screen, I saw that it was a call from my mom. "Please excuse me while I step out to take this call."

"Oh, sure." He stood up and remained standing until I had left the table. What a gentleman!

Chapter 12: Anthony

"Sean. Right?" I had just arrived at the dining hall, and the first person I saw was Sean talking to a female I did not recognize. I recognized him from earlier this week when I was at my wife's chiro appointment.

Turning around at the sound of his name, and then recognizing me, Sean said, "Yeah, man!" He shook my hand, and said, "It's good to see you've made it on out for the retreat."

"Ah, yeah. I was definitely coming. I did not have a choice in the matter. In fact, if I had not, I probably would have never heard the end of it. My wife has been nonstop talking about this event", I paused and looked around the room. "Have you seen her?"

Pointing past me, Sean said, "She is over there getting a drink." Then, he turned in the opposite direction and pointed out the table where they were all sitting. "We are over there. Why don't you set your jacket down and get something eat?"

"Ok." Even though I had plans of taking his advice, I first wanted to kiss my baby. I crossed the room to intersect her path to the table. "Hey there sexy," I said and leaned in to kiss her. When our lips connected, my body temperature began to rise. I swear she melts me every time she touches me. This time was no different. Not wanting to let my thoughts go too gutter, I made myself change focus. I noticed she was balancing a plate, a saucer, and a cup. So, I reached towards her, and asked, "May I help you?"

Sharon smiled softly and answered, "No. I got it Big Daddy. Go ahead and get your food, and I'll see you back at the table", she replied before walking off. I watched her walk away. Pregnancy sure was making her ass look NICE! Yes, sir! Okay, focus. Food.

I headed over to the buffet line, which had shortened during the time I was talking to Sharon. There were five people in front of me. By the time I got into line, it had stopped moving. We had to wait for the servers to bring out more bacon and Belgian waffles. The servers returned within minutes. Once they were out of the way, the line began to move again. I made it through the line, picked up my juice, and headed over to my loving wife.

When I finally made it to the table, Sharon had saved me a seat to the left of her; very befitting. Fore, she is my right hand at all times. As I pulled my chair out, Sharon began introducing me to the group.

"Hey everyone this is my husband, Anthony." They all said some variation of a greeting before Sharon continued, "Anthony, this is Nina, my soror; Kelly, Nina's friend; Stephen, Sean's friend; Sean, you've met him already; and Lisa, Sean's wife."

"Nice to meet all of you. How is the retreat going so far?" I asked as I sat down in the chair next to Sharon. "What all have I missed?"

Sean answered, "You haven't missed much. You are just in time for the best part." Chuckling, he said, "After breakfast, there will be a sex therapist speaking."

"Really?" My eyes got big for a brief moment, and I leaned back in slight disbelief. Then, I turned to my wife, and asked, "What kind of freaky retreat is this?" Everyone at the table burst into laughter.

At that moment, Doc stopped by the table. "Actually, Mr. Lyle, sex therapy is not all about being freaky. Besides, this retreat is not that kind of party", Doc said. "Just make sure you are at the workshop to hear why the sex therapist is here."

"Oh, I plan to be there, Doc!" I called after her. "I do not want to miss this."

Chapter 13: Nina

"It's 9:25. Let's head to the meeting rooms so we can get good seats", I said. I was getting ready to grab my tray and plate, but the men at the table began to collect them.

"You ladies head on down. We'll clean up and meet you there", Stephen said. I was beginning to like him for Kelly. He seemed like a really good guy. Although I had only been around him a little under twenty-four hours, there was still much to learn about him.

Kelly, Lisa, and I stood simultaneously. Sharon took one more swig of her orange juice before she finally stood up.

"Thank you for getting our plates, fellas", I said.

"No problem, ladies", answered Sean. "We will see you in a few minutes."

We turned on our heels and headed towards the exit. Sharon led the way with Lisa beside her. Kelly and I walked side by side. Once we were out of earshot from the men, I bumped Kelly with my right arm.

"So, tell me, Kelly. What do you think about Mr. Wonderful?" I asked. I was being nosy.

Before answering, she shrugged, "I like him, a lot; and he seems to like me a lot. I just can't put my finger on it, but something is making him feel distant. I feel a slight tug of war going on within him. Like I've said, I can tell he likes me, but he seems hesitant about something. I just don't know what it could been." Kelly said.

"Well don't make too much of things right now. Just enjoy his company for the weekend. It is not like you are trying to marry him tomorrow," I told her as we walked down the hallway for the next workshop. Lisa and Sharon were several feet ahead of us. At the doorway of the room, they paused to look behind them, wait for us to catch up.

Lisa called out to us, "hurry up, slow pokes. The seats are filling up quickly.

People were filing into the room quickly. I could tell we were not going to be able to sit together. At best, we can get in a general area, but not all together. We were going to end up split between two rows of seats. The room had been rearranged from the round tables that seated 8 people to auditorium seating. Sharon and Lisa were able to hold two seats for their husbands in their row. Where Kelly and I sat, there was one seat on each side of us. When the fellas came in, Stephen sat next to Kelly, which was not surprising. However, I was surprised by who sat next to me. Marcus Thymes.

My heart skipped a couple of beats. Okay, maybe several beats and now it seemed to be racing to catch up with all the thoughts running through my head. He leaned over until his lips were only inches away from my ear. "Hey, Nina."

The hair on my arms and the back of my neck stood straight up. It took everything in me to act as calmly as possible when I responded, "Hey, Marcus." Then, he flashed that sexy smile. Why is it that he can make me feel this way? And, why in the hell is he even here?!

Kelly leans forward to look around me. When she saw Marcus, her facial expression went from curious to annoyance. Then, she looked at me and said, "You bet not fuck him."

Marcus leans forward and says with a smirk, "What's up, Kelly?"

Kelly rolled her eyes and said, "Go to hell, Marcus." Then, she leaned back in her seat.

Marcus and I dated when I was in college. Although he was eight years older than me, I was so in love with him. I was also a fool for him. Well, it did not start off that way. I was dating someone, and so was he. We were just friends at first. Then, we were friends with benefits. His girlfriend almost caught me at his house once. She never saw me, though. Shamefully, I went out the back door as she came in through the front. I was livid! I was livid, more or less, with myself for getting into a situation like this. I was pissed at him because he was supposed to make sure I was never caught. Although she did not live with him, she just popped up and rang the doorbell. After that happened, I had vowed to never speak to him again. That lasted over a year.

Even though I ended everything, the break up was still hard. I tried to deny that I had fallen in love with him. I missed him terribly. I thought about him more and more as the time passed. When he called over a year later to see how I was doing, naturally, I was fake mad. For a couple of months, he pretended to only want to be friends because he was seeing someone. Yet, occasionally, he would flirt or say something suggestive. It was his way of priming me. I knew it. Sooner than later, he would go for the kill. The next thing I know, we were back to being friends with benefits. He claimed that it was me he really wanted; not her. And, I would believe him. Well, he would never really break up with her, and probably had no plans of doing so either. It was up to me to end things with Marcus. I did not want to play games anymore. Fed up with his games, I ended it. My heart was broken, again. Despite the hurt and emotional rollercoaster, my heart still flip flops for him whenever he is near me.

"You are looking phenomenal," he said, leaning on my shoulder again.

Using my left shoulder, I shrugged him off of me and responded, "And?"

He leaned away from me and said, "No need to have an attitude, baby. I was just paying you a compliment." He raised his hands, palms forward, "I'm come in peace." I rolled my eyes when he smiled at me... or was it a smirk?

"Good morning, everyone!" Doc said loudly as she walked to the podium on the left side of the stage. In the center of the stage was a chiropractic table. "Are you enjoying your morning so far?" *Yeah* echoed throughout the room. "The theme of this year's retreat is Creating Your Inner Peace. There are so many factors that go into creating your inner peace. In my office, we take care of the whole person. Notice, I did not say the whole body. I said, the whole person. To take care of the whole person, we take care of you from the bottom up, top down, and inside out. From the bottom up, we are looking at your structure. From the top down, we are looking at your thoughts and emotions. Lastly, from the inside out, we are looking at the nutrition. Although these entities may appear unrelated to each other, we teach you how much they are intertwined.

"Allow me to give you an example. Imagine you are a person who has unhealthy eating habits and also lives a sedentary lifestyle.

This will lead not only lead to the most obvious result, weight gain, but will also have effects on all eleven systems of the body. As you accumulate fat, the fat has to deposit somewhere. To make room, the skin will stretch. Fat is heavy. As it accumulates, it will weigh down on the muscles. The muscles will respond to the increased weight by tensing up. Any muscle that has long term tension or stress will eventually feel sore or become tender to the touch. So, now you have chronic soreness throughout your body. Have you ever thought about where the muscles attach in your body?

Muscles are attached to the bones in the body. Together, the muscles and skeletal system create movement. However, as your weight increases, not only does it make movement more difficult, it also places more stress on the joints. Stress on the joints can cause the joints to not line properly for use. Because the body has the ability to heal itself, the muscles will tighten up even more to attempt to pull the joints back in place.

Let's not forget that the heart is a muscle. But, I will come back to that.

Instead, let's talk about how this lifestyle affects the nervous system. The nervous system is the boss of the body. It controls everything. The nervous system becomes overwhelmed with information from the nerves telling the brain that various parts of the body is inflamed, injured, and is not working correctly. The nervous system has a sidekick. It is the endocrine system, which controls the hormones. When the nervous system is overwhelmed, the endocrine system will follow suit, and the hormones will be all over the place."

Just then, Doc was interrupted by a male audience member. "I thought that was called PMS!" The room erupted into laughter.

Doc smiled, but continued on, "The lymphatic system becomes clogged. So, now you have swollen lymph nodes and you keep getting sick. The digestive tract is stressed by what you are eating, as well as not eating, and the lack of exercise. Now, you have constipation and is passing horrible gas. The urinary system is angry at you because you hardly drink water. The heart is mad at you, and I mean big mad, because it has to work so much harder to pump blood to the rest of the body. Since the heart is so close to the lungs, the lungs are also big mad because they have to work harder to keep up with the demand for oxygen. With your heart and lungs both having to work harder to keep you alive, now you have high blood pressure. This is just an abbreviated version of what could happen."

Doc continued, "Do you every wonder why the commercials ask is your heart healthy enough for sex? If the blood pressure is high, the body has to prioritize where the blood goes. For some weird reason, the body believes it is more important to send the blood up to the brain than to the penis. There is just something about that line that says, "He died on top of me." The room erupted again with laughter. The Color Purple.

Then, Doc continued, "People tend to handle stress differently. The weight gain can mess with your self-image, self-love, and self-confidence. This, in turn, creates trauma to your thoughts, which affects all of your relationships in some form or fashion. One of your relationships that can be affected by this trauma is the one you have with your significant other. In turn, it can affect your intimacy. In this workshop, we are going to address the effects of chronic stress on one's libido. We have a panel of specialist here with us to cover the different aspects. We have a sex therapist, cardiologist, chiropractor, and a life coach.

"Baby, I miss you," Marcus whispered.

I rolled my eyes, but said nothing because I was really trying to listen to the sex therapist. I also wanted to block him out. Besides, how many times had I heard *'Baby, I miss you'*? The longer he sat next to me, the more annoyed I felt. Interestingly, I could not decide if I was more annoyed with him or myself.

I acknowledge that I am annoyed with him for being so comfortable with taking advantage of the weakness I exhibit in his presence. He knows I am in love with him and want to be with him; he also knows that I know he does not want to commit to me. On the other hand, I am annoyed with myself because I want someone who has shown me, time after time, he does not want me. He wants the benefits of being with me without being with me. It frustrates me that my flesh yearns for the uninhibited pleasure that he gives; because, after the exhilarating moments of raw passion have passed, I feel an emptiness in my soul.

Recently, someone told me, everyone has a *SOUL* account. And, every day is an opportunity to make a deposit; to pour into yourself. You do that by the company you keep, the material you read, the thoughts you feed yourself, and the people you choose to love. Being with Marcus, I was constantly making withdrawals from my soul account. It would not be such a bad thing if Marcus made **regular** deposits back into it. The little bit he would **infrequently** deposit was never enough to keep me for being overdrawn at times. I am tired of paying the overdraft fees of lonely nights and being an afterthought. Now that he is sitting next to me, wanting more from me, it is the perfect time to give him the following message: *You are no longer the soul beneficiary of this account. Access DENIED.*

At the end of the presentation, Marcus stood up with me. I was going to continue ignoring him, but on second thought, I decided to engage him for the last time.

"I did not know you were a patient of Doc." I opened.

"Actually, I am not. My little sister, Michelle, begged me to come. She thinks very highly of Doc. You remember Michelle. Don't you?" he said. He always did do that: say something he thinks I should know because, he recalls saying it; but, does not realize it was something he had spoken to his girlfriend instead of me. How easy it must be to mix us up.

"Uh, no." I began. "I have never met her. But, wait! Remind me again, when would I have had a chance to meet her since we were never really a couple and you never brought me around the family?"

Treating what I had just said like a speedbump, Marcus ignored what I said and kept on with the conversation. "Well, come let me introduce you. She will love you!" Then, he reached for my hand, which I quickly moved out of his reach. The sudden movement shocked him briefly before he smiled, and said, "Come on now, baby. Don't be like that. You know I love you. Do you need a hug?" He opened his arms and began walking towards me to close the one and half foot distance. When he was within my arms' length, reached up with my index finger, placed it in the middle of his forehead, and pushed him backward.

"No!" I said sternly. Then, I enunciated each word carefully, "I do not want to meet your sister or anyone else in your family. I do not want anything from you. Do not call me or text me. Lose my number. This chapter is finished." He backed away from my finger. His expression went from playful to discerning, but he did not speak. I looked him in his eyes one last time. Then, I walked past him. I saw my friend, Kelly, watching from across the room. She had walked off with Stephen after the presentation.

Kelly was standing by the refreshments waiting for me. Everyone was being given a few minutes for a break before the next workshop called *Clean Eating*, which was very befitting since lunch will immediately follow. As I approached, Kelly met me halfway.

"Is everything alright?" she asked.

I answered yes, but Kelly is THAT friend who wanted to make sure.

"Are you sure? Because you know, all you have to do is say the word."

"Yes. I know." I said, and grabbed her arm. "Let's step outside. The air in here is a bit stifling.

Chapter 14: Jennifer

During the Libido presentation, I sat on the end of the front row. I was very interested in learning about how sex therapy helped people. What I was really interested in was what she may have had to say about impotency. However, she did not even touch on the topic; well not with the depth that I was seeking.

After the presentation, I went out into the hallway. There, I saw Nina and Kelly having a conversation. Because I really enjoyed their company, I began to head in their direction. Young people keep me young. At the same time, Sharon and Lisa entered the hallway beside me. So, I tried to fall in stride with her. Simultaneously, I spoke to her, "May I join you?" Since, she had not noticed me on the other side of the doorway when she came out, I startled her.

"Ah!" she shrieked. "Ms. Jennifer, you scared me! Where did you come from," she said. Then, she placed her hand over her racing heart, as if she her hand held the power to calm its rapid beat. The next second, she smiled, and answered, "Of course you can join me."

Together, we maneuvered through the traffic jam that was right in front of the doorway. It wasn't as bad as thought it would be because people are motivated to make way for a person on crutches. And, it didn't hurt that I was 'a senior citizen' too. So, they were very accommodating in making room for us to get through. Don't judge me. When it is convenient to be a senior citizen, I will use it. Otherwise, I am youthful as I feel.

When Sharon, Lisa, and I were upon Nina and Kelly, I could tell by the look on their faces, they had been having a serious conversation, but they changed their expressions after they saw us. I wondered if it had anything to do with the conversation I overheard them having with that young man I saw them with.

"Hey, Nina. Do you mind if I have a private word with you?" I knew it was bold and intrusive of me, but I wanted to speak to her. Although I had only overheard almost all of the conversation, and it probably wasn't my business, I wanted to give her some words of encouragement.

"Sure, Ms. Jennifer." She answered. I gave her the side eye, and she corrected herself. "Jennifer." There was no need for all of that. She followed me to the other side of the hallway where there were only a few people standing around. "What's up, Ms...I mean, Jennifer?"

"I just wanted to pull you aside for a moment to talk to you about the conversation I overheard earlier between you and that young man. Who is he to you? If you don't mind me asking." I said.

"That's a long story. He and I sort of dated off and on for a while, and he is trying to get me to continue on this path with him." She answered.

"What do you mean by 'sort of dated'?" I asked.

"Well, although we have been on a few dates, we mostly smashed." She said. Smashed? What the hell does that mean? Obviously, the look on my face clearly expressed my confusion because she clarified it. "Smashed is slang for having sex. It just sounds better when I say smashed."

It did not sound better. It sounded dumb, but I was not going to press that issue at the moment. What do I know? I am a senior citizen.

"Do you realize that in conducting your relationship with him in this manner, you gave him permission to use you and not see your worth? Sorry to be blunt, but all you were to him was a wet ass. Stop giving up the goods. You are more valuable than that. So, carry yourself in such a way. Let me ask you this, who reached out to whom when you all got together to smash as you call it?" I said.

"It was just about equal. Well, now that I think about it, I reached out the most. I especially did it when I suddenly yearned to be close to him." She answered.

"Today, you were repulsed by him. Right?" I inquired.

"Yes." She was not sure where I was going with this question. So, I continued my line of questions.

"How well do you know your menstrual cycle?" I asked her.

"I think I know it very well. Why?" She responded, even more confused.

"Do you track it on a calendar by chance?" I asked.

"I use a fertility tracker slash cycle tracker app on my phone. It keeps track of my cycle and my ovulation days." She answered.

"Do you mind pulling up the app on your phone? I want to show you something." I said. Without any questioning, she pulled her cellphone out of the case that was on her left hip. She unlocked the screen with a passcode, and tapped the app. When the app opened, she tapped on the tab titled 'calendar'. The days of the month were color coded. There were so many days in pink; so many days in green; and all the rest of the days were gray. The pink days indicated Nina's period. The green days indicated the days she were ovulating. Today was a gray day. She was neither ovulating or on her period, which is why she is able to think more clearly. "Nina, let me let you in on a little secret. While I don't doubt the emotional connection you have to the young man, I am willing to bet that you yearned for him more during those green days. That is because when we are ovulating, our body releases hormones that says 'Come on, baby. I'm ready!' This is when the body is ready to make a baby. You feel sexier during these days and you crave sex. Now that you are aware of that, be smarter, and more vigilant on those days, and avoid him. He doesn't mean you any good. You need to purge him out of your life. When you meet the next guy, don't let sex enter the picture until you have figured out his intentions. It does not take long for a man to let you know what he is really about. If all he wants is sex, he will reveal it. You just have to not ignore the messages he is sending. Do not allow yourself to be in denial, and do not allow yourself to try to make him into the man you want him to be. Ok, Nina?" I said.

Nina wiped a few tears from her eyes before she nodded her head. "Ok. I will do better. I need to act like I know my worth, and start walking in my glory. Thank you, Jennifer. I needed to hear that." She leaned in, and gave me a hug.

"Wipe your eyes. We don't want them thinking I was over here beating you up." I said with a smile.

"But weren't you?" She smiled. After she wiped her face, we returned to where the ladies were waiting patiently.

Chapter 15: Lisa

"We should go see the therapist when we get back to the Lou", Sean whispered into my ear. Oh, yeah? Why am I not the least bit of surprised to hear him say this? Then, again, I am a little bit surprised. Did he think we have intimacy issues? I did not think we had any. I thought we were fine. Would we be there for enhancements? If that was the case, then, I was definitely game. We could always venture to the next level...whatever that may be.

Feigning surprise, I responded, "Oh?!" I thought I would play along with this conversation to see where it would go. "Why, Baby?"

"Well, why not?" he responded with a raised eyebrow and a slight head tilt to the left. I immediately knew why he was asking. It was for mere entertainment just to see what it was like to see a sex therapist.

I rolled my eyes, and said, "We'll see." Excitedly, he kissed me on my lips before turning to see where the guys were standing. If you could have seen his face at that moment, you would have thought I had just told him to take me right here, right now. All I could do was shake my head.

"Baby, I'm going over here with the guys. See you in a little while?" When I nodded, he took off. Once again, I shook my head and smiled.

I looked past Sean and saw Nina and Kelly in the hallway walking together. They were not too far ahead. So, I started walking faster to catch up to them. As I walked through the doorway, Sharon appeared at my left elbow. "Hey, Lisa. Have you seen Nina and Kelly?" she said.

"Hey! I was just making my way over to them." I nodded in their direction, and said, "They are ahead of us. Let's catch them." Just then, Jennifer appeared beside Sharon, startling her. Together, we excused our way through the crowd until we were within earshot of them and I could call out to them. "Nina! Kelly!"

Hearing their name, they turned to see who was calling them. Nina spotted us first. Then, she motioned for Kelly to step off to the side to wait for us. Once Kelly was off to the side, she was able to see us in the crowd.

"Hey, ladies!" I said when we finally caught up to them.

"Hey", they said simultaneously.

"Did you all enjoy the therapist?" I asked.

"I sure did. I had no idea what a sex therapist was before today. I also didn't understand how important heart health was regarding a healthy libido. Although the last seminar was very interesting, I am more excited about this food workshop coming up next," answered Nina.

"Me, too!" Sharon added.

At that moment, Jennifer whispered something in Nina's ear. Then, they walked off in private. "We will be back," Jennifer called over her should as they stepped away from the group.

For the past twenty-four hours, the ladies and I have been getting to know each other. Jennifer, was the oldest in the group, and I was interested in learning her story. Just by looking at her, you could tell she has a story, or a hundred. When she and Nina came back from their private conversation, I decided to change the focus of the conversation from the upcoming workshop to Jennifer.

"So, Jennifer." Hearing me call her name over Sharon's voice startled Jennifer, but everyone turned in response. "The ladies and I have been sharing our "What brought us to Doc" stories amongst each other, and I was wondering what your story is. What sent you to the Doc, if you don't mind sharing?"

Visibly caught off guard, Jennifer stammered. "Uh, what?" The color even seemed to drain from her face briefly. Quickly, she collected her thoughts, and answered, "There are so many reasons I have gone to see Doc. I'll share one of them with you before the weekend ends"

I calmly answered, "Please, don't take offense. I was only asking because we had been sharing our stories, and we were just curious. For example, one of was trying to perform sexy chair dance for her man and ended up on the floor. Not because her man laid her there, I might add." Everyone chuckled, before I continued. "Then, another one of us tried to duplicate a sexy shower scene they had probably seen in a movie, we shall say. She ended up on her back, but not quite how she had imagined she would." This time, everyone hollered.

"Well!" Jennifer exclaimed. "Not only are you all the class clowns in the circus, but you also like to do stunts! What a talented crew!" She laughed some more. Somberly, she said, "I'm not quite ready to share a story yet. Eventually, I will share."

I smiled, nodded, and said, "Let's go outside or at least get out of this congested hallway."

We all stepped outside into the late morning sun. There was a soft light breeze coming off of the lake. It had me wishing I had not left my jacket in my room. My rayon top was not enough of a barrier against the wind.

Kelly broke the silence that had enveloped us when we were inside the lobby. "This place is so beautiful and quiet. I actually can hear myself think. You know, I would not mind coming back here alone for a weekend getaway. Nina, I really do appreciate you convincing me to come along. I am definitely enjoying myself."

"Hey, I am glad you came. It was something different from your routine. Plus, I'm very proud of my chiropractor, and I wanted you to meet her." Nina replied.

"Wait! You've never been adjusted by Doc?!" Sharon directed towards Kelly. "You are missing out! What are you waiting on? Girl, if only you knew what you were missing out on! It is the best thing ever! I stay adjusted."

"How often do you have to get adjusted," Kelly asked.

Sharon answered, "I don't have to get adjusted, but I choose to get adjusted once a week."

"Once a week?!" Kelly shrieked. "So, it is true that once you start going, you have to keep going! Yeah, I'm not getting adjusted. I don't want to start something I have to keep doing forever."

"Wait, wait, and wait! Calm down. Once you get an adjustment, you do not have to keep going forever. However, after you start going, you will WANT to keep it apart of your routine because you feel so good afterwards," Sharon responded. Then, I added to the conversation.

"While you are getting your panties in a bunch about getting chiropractic adjustments, I bet you didn't complain about how often you were going to have to put gas in your car when you first purchased your car. Did you? Nope. But, you continue gassing up the car because you enjoy riding around in it. It's the same thing with chiropractic. I keep going because it makes me feel good and allow me to the things that make me happy," I said.

Kelly looked down at her watch, and sarcastically said, "Wow! Where did the time go?! It looks like we need to head back inside the lodge." We all laughed. Kelly reached for the door handle, and held the door open. As we walked through the door, I heard her say, "Whew! That was serious." I simply chuckled.

When we entered the lobby, Sharon turned right to take the stairs down to the dining hall. As we filed into the dining hall, we saw Doc standing behind a podium, patiently waiting for everyone to take a seat. For some reason, this seminar was little less populated. I guess everyone was more interested in listening to the sex therapist than learning about eating cleanly; or they could be traumatized by last night's dinner.

"Welcome back!" Doc began. "I hope you all enjoyed listening to the panelists." The audience clapped their hands in agreement. Doc smiled, and continued, "In this session, we are going to talk about the significance of eating clean. Eating cleanly is an extremely important component to creating inner peace. Any and everything you can think of has an energy associated with it. When creating your inner peace, you seek out positive energies. Typically, you want to surround yourself with positive things. If you want positivity to radiate from you, you must put positive things inside you i.e. positive thoughts, images, and food. The cleaner you eat, the better you feel.

"There are many signs that you are in a chronic state of inflammation. Start by looking at your skin. Do you seem to keep having skin eruptions such as acne or eczema? Do you have frequent allergic reactions? Signs of chronic inflammation can show up in your gut, also known as your digestive tract. Do you frequently have abdominal cramping? What about acid reflux? Are you gassy, constipated, or having diarrhea? Do you constantly have headaches?" Doc explained.

Doc picked up the mic and walked to the other side of the audience. "So, what kind of food are considered inflammatory? Think of the acronym CRAP, which stands for Carbonated, Refined, Artificial, and Processed things. If carbonated drinks are your beverages of choice, lose it. Those drinks are full of sugar. Sugar is inflammatory. Drink water. Let's talk about refined foods. Examples of refined foods are your breads and pastas. Get rid of the bread and pastas. It swells you up and causes you to hold water. Let's talk artificial, which is almost everything at the grocery stores. The products that do not have artificial components are you fruits, vegetable, nuts, some meats, and poultry. Say goodbye to anything that has a long shelf life. This now leads me to processed foods. Processed foods have a whole lot of salt in them. When you see CRAP, do not walk away; run away."

Someone raised their hand. Doc acknowledged them, "Yes?"

"So what is there to eat?" he asked.

"Eat fruits, vegetables, nuts, fish, and chicken", she answered.

"What about the meat?" he asked.

"Pork is terrible for you. It raises your blood pressure. Stay away from it. So goodbye to sausage and bacon. Eat red meat sparingly. Instead of beef, try lamb." Doc responded.

"I like shrimp and lobsters", he said.

"Sparingly, but really not at all. Shrimp are bottom-feeders and so is catfish. You really should not be eating them." Doc responded. "Eating cleanly gives your body the proper fuel it needs to work efficiently. Food is supposed to be fuel for the body, not poison. Do not live to eat; eat to live.

The guy responded for the last time, "In other words, starve to death. You just named everything I love to eat."

A woman in the back of the room raiser her hand. "Yes?" Doc answered.

"Doc, I have been eating those fruits, vegetables, fish and chicken. Yet my weight lost has hit a plateau. What could it be?" she asked.

Doc responded, "What kind of fruits are you eating?"

"Well, I often eat grapes, watermelon, honeydew melon, strawberries, and occasionally banana and apples", the woman said.

"When you are trying to lose weight, you have to be very careful about your sugar intake. Sugar is everywhere, naturally and otherwise. The fruits you are eating often have a lot of sugar in them. Why do you eat grapes, watermelon, and honeydew?" Doc said.

"Because they taste good," she answered Doc.

"They taste good because they are…" Doc said, prompting the woman to fill in the blank, which she did.

"Sweet."

"Exactly. Since you are trying to lose weight, cut back on your sugar even more. Remove the banana, which you say you hardly ever eat. Simply do not eat it. Do not eat any type of melons. Say goodbye to watermelon, honeydew melon, and cantaloupe, although you did not mention it. Eat apples, oranges, strawberries, blueberries, blackberries, and raspberries. Of course drink plenty of water. Drink at least half your body weight in ounces of water. If you weigh 164 pounds, your need to drink at least eighty-two ounces of water. I know they say drink eight cups of water a day, but depending on your size, you may need more than eight cups." Doc answered, then continued her presentation on clean eating and the benefits. "If you do not want to cut your sugary intake, then you need to increase your cardio."

Sitting in this workshop made me realize just how messed up my diet was. I can definitely do better. I need to change my lifestyle. I want my body to be the best that it can; and I do not mean appearance wise. That will come as a result of my lifestyle. I mean, I want my organs to work as best as they can. I want to stay alive and have a great quality of life. I am less likely to be sick and have health problems if I eat right and exercise.

As Doc came to the end of her presentation, you can see the audience getting antsy. All of that talk about food had made everyone ready for lunch. We were ready to eat. At that moment, I realized no food had been brought out for the buffet that I had assumed we were going to have. So where was lunch?

"Ladies and gentleman, we have a surprise for you", Doc began. "Lunch will be done a little differently this year. We teamed up with a brilliant chef to give you an experience with clean eating that you will not soon forget. He has created a three course meal that will tantalize all of your senses. Please, put your hands together for your chef, Holfwang Puck!"

The dining hall erupted in cheers. In my best Kevin Harts' voice impersonation, I said, "It's about to go down."

Chapter 16: Nina

"Holfwang?!" I exclaimed as I looked around the table at the ladies. I could not conceal my excitement. Indulging in great tasting cuisines is one of my favorite things to do! I remember the first time I ate at one of his restaurants. Kelly and I had gone to Disney World down in Orlando, Florida for the Disney's Princess Half Marathon we were running. The food was orgasmic good.

"This is wonderful! I'm really glad you convinced me to come on this retreat", said Kelly.

Just then, servers began bringing out the first course. It was a kale salad with grill artichoke. It looked delicious! After everyone had been served, Sharon blessed the food, the hands that had prepared the meal, and all the hands that will received the meal. For several minutes, there was nothing but silence as we savored our salad.

At last, Sharon said, "So, Nina, I do not recall you sharing your story as to what sent you to Doc. Do you mind sharing?"

I finished chewing, and wiped my mouth before answering her. "Well, no. I do not mind. We have all been quite candid this weekend. So, I will share my story." I paused before starting because the servers were clearing the table for the next course. I waited until after the server placed the last plate on the table. The next course was curried chicken sautéed with fresh mint-soy vinaigrette and steamed asparagus.

I began, "Well, Sharon, several weeks before you referred me to Doc, I had had an SRI." Everyone at the table said "SRI?" at the same time.

"What in the hell is an SRI?" asked Lisa.

"An SRI is an acronym I learned from Doc when I told her how I injured myself. She told me SRI stands for Sexually Related Injury." Our table erupted in laughter, drawing all attention from the people at neighboring tables. "Shhhhhh!"

Laughing, I went on with my story. The ladies all leaned in as far as they could to keep from missing anything I said.

I continued, "If I had to title my story, I would call it the 'Jawbreaker.'"

Lisa interjected, "I'm dead" while everyone else snickered.

"Kelly and I had been out at a restaurant one day, and I had just finished telling her how much "I love, love, love food!" Kelly joined in, all the while mimicking my voice. I am sure she remembers this story like it was yesterday. "Anyway! I wish I could get paid to try new dishes at restaurants. That would be the life for me", I said.

"Kelly and I usually get together every Wednesday for lunch. This particular day we had gone to Steak and Shake. While I was sipping on my Strawberry Banana, side-by side milkshake, she decides to ask me about my then beau who had recently proposed to me. She said, *'Have you finally broken down and given him some head yet? I can't believe this is not an issue for him.'"* Just then, Sharon and Lisa fell out laughing. I side eyed them, and rolled my eyes before continuing. "Anyway, when Kelly asks me this, I am swearing that her voice is carrying. So, Kelly says, *'Girl! First of all, no one can hear me. Second, you are probably the only person in here not giving head. And third, answer the question: Did you finally give him some?'"* They were laughing so hard.

I continued, "She was wondering because I had been telling her how my fiancée had been asking me to do it for a while. He had even refrained from oral on me because I wouldn't reciprocate. As great as it made me feel, and as fair as his request was, I could not get with it; until the morning of our weekly lunch date. I had finally decided to give it a try on my fiancée. I won't go into details, but afterwards, my jaw was sore and tender to the touch. A novice, I figured this was the usual occupational hazard associated with this line of work, and assumed it will soon go away. My jaw was just tired from an unusual workout." They hollered.

"So, I went on with the rest of my morning, otherwise feeling awesome. I was smiling and walking on air. Both lips had gotten a good morning kiss that day", I said.

"Well, alright now!" said Lisa. "That is how a woman is supposed to wake up. Minus the jaw pain, that is. You need to work on that." Snapping her fingers three times, she said, simultaneously, "Practice, practice, practice. Surely, your fiancée will appreciate it."

Sharon and Kelly were crying laughing. Sharon was laughing so hard that she was leaning over and grabbing her side with laughter, and trying to catch her breath.

"Anyway! During lunch, my jaw pain worsened. For lunch, I had ordered the 7x7 burger, which is a very tall burger. Even after smashing that burger down as far as I could, I still had to open my mouth wide to get the sandwich in my mouth. When I did, I felt a pop in my right jaw. This was the second time I had felt it since that morning, but it was a lot worst this time. The pop was so painful that it brought tears to my eyes. Seconds later, my ears started hurting. I had continued having pain for several weeks until after Sharon encouraged me to go see Doc." Turning to Sharon, "Thank you."

Only briefly, Sharon stopped laughing, gave me a serious look, and said, "I'm just glad I could help a sister out", Sharon said. Then, she laughed so more.

I had finished my story just in time for dessert, which was the Almond Granita. It was such a nice and sweet way to end lunch.

Jennifer shook her head and laughed, "Amateurs."

Chapter 17: Jennifer

"Well," I began as dessert was being served. I guess my voice startled everyone at the table, because they all looked surprised to hear me. Sharon's eyebrows were raised in anticipation of what I was getting ready to say next. "I'm ready to share my story. Let me say this, because I have been going to the chiropractor for many years, there have been many reasons why I have had to go to Doc. However, there was this one period in my life when I made getting my adjustments less of a priority. I was doing all that I do on a regular basis without getting the necessary tune up my body needed. My body was starting to hurt constantly, but I still didn't get to the chiropractor. On top of everything that was going on, I was constantly traveling for my job; flying across the country. "

"Is that right?" Lisa asked. Then, she leaned in and said, "Do tell us more."

Pacing myself, I ate another bite of my Almond Granita, and then said, "If I had to title my story, I would call it. Impotency."

Kelly's face fell. Then she tilted her head slightly to the right and, in disbelief, repeated what I said, "Impotency. How did THAT send you to Doc?"

"I was suffering from primary and secondary impotency, but did not know it at the time. The guy I was dating at the time was a great guy, but I was beginning to have very little desire to have sex with him." I answered.

Nina asked, "Were you not attracted to him anymore?"

"Oh! No! That was not the problem. I absolutely found him very attractive. He was super sexy to me. He was a chiseled, tall, chocolate skinned brother with pretty white teeth. He had a slight gap between his top front teeth. He even has full luscious lips. Yet, having sex with him had become a chore. It was painful. He tried to be as gentle as possible, but it would still hurt." I continued as our dessert plate were being cleared from the table. Looking around, I could see people were beginning to clear out, though we continued to sit.

"Dayum!" said Nina. "He must be a muthaflipping monster!" Everyone laughed. Nina had verbalized what everyone else was thinking.

"No. Comment." I said, stressing each word.

"THIS is intriguing. Primary impotency. Let me make sure I understand. Because you were in constant pain all over, your sexual desire was non-existent?" Nina said. She shook her head in disbelief. "That's rough. I simply cannot imagine being in so much pain for such a length of time that it affects my sex drive."

"Well, it did. My body was hurting from head to toe. One of the problems I had was a nagging earache. I went to every doctor except my chiropractor for the ear pain. I would swear I was experiencing an ear infection. Yet, every time my ears were checked, I was told they were clear. It seemed like my allergies never let up. I always had pain around my eyes. Sometimes, out of nowhere, my vision would become blurry. I thought it was due to aging or that I needed prescription lens. I tried my best to ignore my pain, but I could not. One day, I bought myself some stronger readers. That did not help a thing." I paused a moment, to sip water from my glass that the waiter was getting ready to take as he cleaned the tables .

"Those things you mentioned sound like common issues. I don't understand why those things would affect your sexual drive," Kelly stated.

"Well, the eye pain, blurriness, and earache were giving me frequent headaches. I was not getting any relief from any of the over the counter medications. The doctor prescribed me some pain pills. They, too, were not very helpful. So, there were nights when I became THAT female who says, '*Not tonight, honey. I have a headache*'", I answered. The only thing on my mind was my constant pain.

"Oh, wow", responded Kelly. "Was there any other physical pain?"

"Was there any other pain?!" I asked incredulously. "That was enough in and of itself. However, the list was longer. My guy was much taller than me. Giving him a hug while standing had dropped to the bottom of my list of things to do with him. To reach above my head was a chore. Reaching upward caused pain in my shoulders, neck, and lower back. When he would come in for a hug, I would cringe; anticipating the pain. If he was excited about anything, and came towards me with great speed, I would have to brace myself."

"That sounds miserable." Lisa said. Sharon elbowed Lisa. Lisa looked at her and mouthed the word 'what'.

Lisa looked around at everyone and said out loud, "What?! Well, it does! I'm just saying." Then, she shrugged her shoulders.

"She's right! I was miserable. Pain had become my lifestyle."

"I'm super curious. What made the act of sex painful? Or not desirable? I thought sex get rid of headaches." Nina inquired.

"Well, for him to lie on top of me was terrible. The weight of his frame would hurt my breast and stomach. Let me tell you about the breast soreness! He would barely have one in his hand, let alone his mouth, and I would cringe. Sometimes, I would bite my lips and suck it up for his enjoyment. I was taking one for the team baby. I could not wait for him to finish. Since my hips were already super sore, spreading them was not a movement I looked forward to. They ached so much. I would tighten up my thighs, trying to ease the impact of his pelvic thrust. This would block him from giving me deep penetration...that is until my thighs went weak. And, another reason I had very little desire was the fact I was always exhausted. I had what doc called chronic fatigue. Sometimes I was plain ole too sleepy to even think about sex."

"That is rough!" said Lisa.

"Please excuse me for sounding rude," Kelly said, "but I'm going to state the obvious. It never crossed my mind that you were even sexually active." At first, there was a grave silence. The others really could not believe Kelly actually said anything. Sure the other ladies had been thinking it, but probably was not going to say anything in my presence. After what seemed like an eternity, everyone looked at me.

Returning their gaze, I replied, "Well." Following a pregnant pause, I said, "Even with my one leg can I still wrap my leg around his head. My leg was amputated; not my vagina. Geesh!"

Relieved, everyone laughed.

"Well, back to my story. When I saw Doc for the first time after having been away so long, I could barely stand for Doc to touch my skin because I hurt so badly. Please don't be mistaken. Just because I could barely stand to be touched, that is no indication of Doc being rough with me. In fact, she could not have been anymore gentler. She even adjusted me with a very gentle technique. All I had to do was lie face down on the table and relax while she held her thumb underneath a ligament or something for about fifteen minutes or more. It was so gentle, I fell asleep on the table."

"A thumb under a ligament? That's different. Doc must not have done that technique on me. I've never just laid on a table while she has adjusted me. Usually, I am responding to a command she was giving me and lifting my legs," said Nina.

"Well, seeing I have only one leg, I'm will to bet that is why she does not use that technique on. I'm just guessing," I responded to Nina.

"Where is this ligament?" asked Lisa.

"In the weirdest place ever; my butt cheek." I answered.

The ladies burst into laughter.

"Interesting!" Nina said. "I can only imagine how awkward that would have been had that been how she adjusted me on the first visit."

"You know what? Doc does a fabulous job of explaining to you what she is going to do before she does it. She even pulls out a book to show you pictures. HOWEVER, it was still awkward as hell! I mean, think about it. Most of the time, when you go see a medical doctor, you sit across from the doctor, have a conversation, usually very brief, maybe you are touched on the area of complaint, and then maybe given a prescription. In other words, there is minimal contact when I go to the doctor. So, imagine my shock when I learned that chiropractic was so hands on. Has Doc ever told you what the word 'chiropractic' meant" I paused to see if anyone knew the answer. No one was anxious to give an answer. So, I answered my own question. "Don't quote me, but Doc said something to the effect of, chiropractic comes from "chiro", meaning hands, and "practice", meaning practical. Together, those words mean done by hand.

"Well, despite the awkwardness, when I got off of the table, I was amazed at how much better I was feeling after one treatment. Now, when I say 'feeling better', I mean relative to how I felt when I first came through the door. I was not one hundred percent, and I knew I was going to need more treatment; for which I came back regularly for about a month.

"After a few weeks of treatment, my body became less and less sensitive to touch and pressure; and Sex was not as much of a physical chore. Now, it was more of a mental chore. My career obligations were now affecting our relationship. I was at the height of my career. I was very close to achieving my goals. All I could think about was my career. Not enjoying playing second fiddle to my career, he grew tired of it, and we eventually parted ways. Fast forward to today. I have not had any of those issues at all. Because I stay adjusted and exercise, my sex life is very much active."

Everyone's eyes grew large in surprise. Though, unsurprisingly, Kelly said what everyone was thinking, "As old as you are, you are still sexually active?"

"Kelly, honey, yes. And, when he plans to be behind me while I'm standing, I am certain to put on my work boot, which stays beside the bed." I said, just to mess with the young blood.

"Work boot?" Kelly asked.

"Yes, work boot. Work boots have a thick rubber sole that are slip resistant. I have to practice safety in all matters." I said. They just laughed!

The ladies and I were now the last ones remaining in the room. So, we gathered our things and filed out of the room and into the hallway.

"We can finish this conversation in the lobby," Lisa suggested as she slid her arms into her sweater.

"That is a great idea," Sharon chimed in. "Besides, there is a nice fireplace in the lobby where we can sit next to. I have a chill anyway." She led the way, and we all followed her. Nina and I brought up the rear. She walked along side me as I hopped along. As we moved through the hallway, Nina asked me THE question: What high school did you graduate from? I wasn't expecting the question, so it took me longer than a moment to respond. We both laughed at the implications.

Simple, though the question may seem, its history is deep. In the late 1800s and early 1900s, the answer to that simple question allowed people to draw conclusions about where you lived and your socioeconomics. Yet, Nina and I laughed. We were making light of the question. I answered, "I graduated from a Catholic, all girl high school. And you?"

"I graduated from Gateway City Public High School. Thanks for humoring me," she said.

Our walk to the lobby was a short walk. Upon arrival, we saw many retreat attendees hanging around, but none of them chose to occupy the seats near the fireplace. I sat down in an oversized chair and placed my crutches beside it on the floor. The heat from the fire felt so good against the palms of my hands, which I held out towards the fire.

There were only four oversized chairs around the fireplace. Since Kelly did not claim one for herself, she decided to prop up against the arm of the chair that Nina was sitting in. She chose the side of the chair that was closest to me.

"Ms. Jennifer, you are so hilarious! I'm so glad to have met you." Kelly wasted no time getting back into my story.

"Hey, Ant!" Sean called out to me. "Do you mind if I call you Ant?" he asked once he was beside me.

I had been standing in the hallway just outside of the dining hall when he approached me. "No, I don't mind. It's cool if you call me Ant. That what my friends call me." I answered. "Besides, it seems we might become good friends anyway." Just then, my phone vibrated in my pocket. It was a text message from Sharon telling me she was with the ladies, and she will catch up with me at the next workshop.

"How are you enjoying the weekend so far? You know, with this being your first time and all?" he asked.

"In the short time I've been here, I'd say it has been pretty cool. I have learned a lot about finding my inner peace." I said sarcastically. Sean laughed.

"Give it more time. It should eventually come around for you. About the inner peace, man, listen, it makes a big difference in the results when the doctor looks at all aspects when treating you. Your care is truly customized." We saw Stephen come out of the men's room. Sean lightly tapped my shoulder, and said, "Why don't you join us. We have about forty-five minutes until the next presentation. We are heading down to the rec room to shoot pool. Do you play?"

Perking up, I responded, "Do I play? Man, Eight ball is my middle name." I said. Little did he know, pool was my hustle during the college days. That was how I paid for books and kept food in my belly. Although it was a dangerous means for money, I really enjoyed the game.

"Well let's go." Noticing Stephen looking around for him, Sean waved his right arm overhead until he caught Stephen's attention. Stephen walked over to us while zipping his jacket.

Now standing beside me, and across from Sean, he said, "I'm ready."

Sean nodded his head, and began leading the way out of the lobby and onto the porch of the lodge. Sean reached the door and held it open for us to walk through.

When we stepped outside, the sun was high in the sky and kicking off some serious heat for October. Earlier this morning, the temperatures were cooler, accompanied by a chilly breeze off of the lake. My long sleeved shirt had been perfect for that weather. Now, with the absence of the breeze and the warmer temperatures, I did not need the shirt. According to my Apple watch, the temperature was eighty degrees. Fortunately, I had another shirt underneath. So, I took off the long sleeved shirt while I walked slightly behind Sean and Stephen. Once it was off, I draped it over my arm and picked up my pace until I fell in step with them.

When we got to the rec room, there was only one table open. We hurried over to it before anyone else could claim it. Stephen racked the balls while Sean and I grabbed our cues. After the balls were racked, Stephen went over to the wall to choose a cue. On his way back to the table, Stephen asked, "Who is going to lag first?"

Sean and I looked at each other. Nodding towards Sean, I said, "You can shoot first."

"Ok", he said. Sean stood at the head of the table and placed the cue ball down. He leaned over the ledge of the table and struck the cue ball. The ball ran down the side of the table towards the foot of the table, where it hit the edge, and rolled back towards the head. When the ball reached the head, it bounced off the ledge softly and stopped just in front of the second dot. Stephen went next. His shot stopped just behind the second dot, making him the first shooter between Sean and himself. Then, it was my turn. I stroked the cue ball just right. It stopped half way between the first and second dots. The order of the players was me, Stephen, and then Sean.

"I see you. I see you." Stephen said.

I offered a half smile, and said, "I'll take balls one through five; Stephen will take six through ten; and Sean will take eleven through fifteen. Let's play", I said. I bent down and leveled my eyes with the cue ball. Just before I took my shot, I asked "Are we calling shots?"

Sean spoke up quickly, "Naw, my man. I'm not that good, and I want a fighting chance."

"Ok." That was a good call. Or else, I would have embarrassed them if they had agreed to call shots. On the break, I sank two balls on the first shot; one in each corner pocket. The four ball went in the left corner pocket and the twelve went in the right corner pocket.

"Alright. I see you." Stephen said again.

On the next shot, I sank the ten ball in the left corner pocket, but scratched on the next shot. Sean and Stephen were able to return one their balls to the table. Then, it was Stephen's turn. He sank two of my balls, and one of Sean's before he accidentally sank one of his own balls. Sean and I both returned one of our balls to the table. Next, it was Sean's turn. He was much better than he had led me to believe. He sunk three more balls from both Stephen's and my set. I was beginning to worry until he had fouled. He hit a ball off the table. Stephen and I both returned one of our balls. It was my turn again. At that moment, I said to myself 'Let me play for real for real'. I cleaned the table of all the balls in their set. After I sank the last ball, I smiled and stood up. I looked over at Sean and Stephen, and said, "Good game." I said.

Shaking his head, Sean said "Yeah, good game." He looked down at this watch to check the time. "The next presentation begins in ten minutes. We might as well head back over to the lodge. We grabbed our belongings and walked towards the entrance of the rec center.

On the way out of the door, I decided to share my happy news. "Hey. Does either of you have any children?" I asked as I held the door open for them. Stephen answered first as he cleared the threshold.

"Nope. Not yet; but one day." Stephen said.

Then, Sean answered, "Same here." Redirecting the question at me, he asked, "What about you and Sharon?"

"We have recently learned that we are pregnant again." I answered.

"Well, congratulations on baby number what?" Sean asked.

Walking towards the main lodge placed the sun directly in our faces. I pulled my shades out of my jacket pocket, and put them on before responding. "Actually, this is our second pregnancy. We miscarried during the first pregnancy. We took our loss pretty hard because we really wanted to start building our family. Man, it took us awhile to heal. We even had to get counseling. As we embark on this journey again, we are really praying we have an uneventful pregnancy and deliver a healthy baby boy or girl."

The walk from the rec center was shorter than I remembered it being. Wanting to continue enjoying the fresh air, we stopped at the base of the steps leading up to the entrance of the lodge to chat a little longer.

Stephen spoke. "Wow, man! First of all, congratulations to you and Sharon. And, I definitely pray you have a better outcome this go round."

"Same here," Sean agreed.

"Thanks!" We stood in silence for a brief moment, each of us lost in our own thoughts. Then, I broke the silence, "Might as well go in."

As we entered the lodge, I heard my wife's voice. She was sitting in one of the oversized chairs by the fireplace with the ladies. Deeply engrossed in their conversation, none of them noticed us walking up on them until we were right next to them. I leaned down and whispered in her ear, "I've been missing you, beautiful. How is our baby doing?" She smiled warmly, and then turned her head up to kiss me.

"I've missed you too", she whispered. After letting her gaze briefly drop towards her stomach, she looked up at me, and whispered, "Our baby is doing well." As we had our private conversation, I saw Stephen moving over to Kelly, who was sitting on the edge of Nina's chair. He leaned down, and whispered in her ear. It was obviously pleasant because it brought a smile to her face. They do make a rather handsome couple if I must say so myself.

The ladies began to scoot to the edge of their chairs, preparing to stand. I held my hand out for Sharon to grab so I can help her up. Not paying any attention to my outstretched hand, she attempted to stand on her own. When she shifted her weight to stand, she fell backwards into the chair. Her right foot had not been planted very well, and it slipped out from under her. "Are you ok," I asked.

"Yes", she answered. This time, she noticed my hand. She planted her feet more firmly, and grabbed my hand, and stood up successfully.

While I helped Sharon up, Sean helped Lisa and then Jennifer. Once Lisa was up on her feet, she said, "Let's head to the next seminar. Why don't we all sit together?" said Lisa. Everyone nodded and prepared to follow her. Lisa led the way with Sean beside her. Behind them were Kelly and Stephen. Sharon, Nina, Jennifer, and I pulled up the rear. We carried on separate conversations as we slowly walked towards the meeting rooms. When we arrived, we were one of the first ones there. Therefore, there was a plethora of seats from which to choose. We chose the first row; front and center.

After sat beside my wife, I wrapped my arm around Sharon shoulders, pulled her towards me, and planted a kiss on her forehead. "I just love you so much. I am very excited about our pregnancy. But, I will admit that I am scared. I mean, I know each pregnancy is different; and I know a lot of things are different about our circumstances this time, but that doesn't stop me from worrying a little bit. Talk to me baby. How are you feeling?"

Sharon lifted her face to look into my eyes. Her eyes were glassy, but the tears never left them. She took a deep breath before answering, "I think about our first baby a lot. I really do. I have tortured myself with many 'what ifs'. As we anticipate the arrival of this baby, I am hopeful. I am even more hopeful because of what Doc has shared with me about chiropractic and having a healthy pregnancy and delivery. The energy I feel is so overwhelmingly positive. We will be okay. I know we will." She squeezed my hand in reassurance.

The room was filling up quickly. People were returning from lunch. They were quite loud as they conversed and shared some laughs. Doc emerged from the crowd and walked towards the microphone where her assistant was doing an audio check. She spoke a few words to him and then turned her attention on us.

"Good afternoon, everyone! Did you enjoy lunch?" 'Yeah' echoed throughout the room. "This afternoon, we are going to talk about *Posturing Yourself for Inner Peace*. You may be doing all of the other things to create inner peace, but your body has to be in the proper position to receive it. What are you talking about Doc? Thanks for asking." Doc said. The audience laughed at Doc asking herself a question and answering it.

"Have you ever heard of the saying, *Posturing yourself for success?* That simply means you cannot expect to be successful or to be the best at what you want to do if you do not position yourself to receive it. Just as you have to position yourself for success, you have to position yourself for inner peace."

Doc walked over to Lisa and stood in front of her. "Lisa, please hold your right hand out." Lisa did it. Close your hand." Lisa did. "Lisa, can you receive this one dollar bill I have in my hand if your hand is closed?" When Doc put the microphone in front of her mouth, the room was able to hear her respond, "No."

"Exactly! The same goes for your body. If the body is hunched over, and you are shrinking into yourself because of pain, you are blocking your inner peace. People who are hunched over are in some kind of distress. How many people do you know that has chronic pain and have inner peace? Probably none. People with chronic pain are not the happiest people. People who are their healthiest, pain free, and have inner peace stand tall and erect with their chest up and out. This workshop will teach you how chiropractic adjustments can help you improve your posture, and receive the inner peace you deserve." Doc said.

As I sat listening, I began thinking about my own inner peace; more specifically, my posturing. I have noticed that my shoulders were rounding inward these days. I even think I am starting to shrink a little. Until recently, I had never really seen a need to go to a chiropractor. It wasn't like I was in any pain. However, I have been noticing things like chronic muscle tightness. Interesting. I may just have to check Doc out when I get back. I know Sharon will be happy to hear that. I looked over at my wife with a smile and placed my right hand on top of her left knee. Lovingly, she squeezed my hand and returned the smile.

Doc continued her presentation. I was surprised to learn how much information she is able to acquire about a person from a spinal examination. She said the spine is made up of twenty-four moveable bones called vertebrae. There are openings on both sides of each vertebra through which nerves travel. Each nerve go to a specific area, or organ in the body. All of that meant absolutely nothing to me until me she explained how aches, pain, and chronic muscle tension correlates with the symptoms we experience but do not realize are related.

Doc asked for a volunteer to demonstrate how the body tells all. A young lady named, Alicia, volunteered; and she had never been to a chiropractor before. Doc asked her if she had anything bothering her. The young lady said her neck, the top part of her back by her shoulders, and her lower back. That sounded like almost everything to me. Doc asked the young lady to lie face down on the chiropractic table.

The table was about three feet high above the ground, and about six and a half feet long with an oval opening at the head of the table. The opening was about fourteen inches long by four inches wide to allow the patient to be able to breathe while face down. On each side of the table, just below the head piece, there were short platforms for patients to rest their arms.

When the young lady laid down, Doc walked to the foot of the table. Then, she placed her hands on the lady's feet to check something. I assume watching the feet must be very important, because there was a video camera aimed at Alicia's heels, which allowed the audience to see them. We could see that the right leg was about a half an inch shorter than the left. When Doc swiped her hand across the legs, we saw the leg react. What kind of magic is this? Doc continued placing her hand on different areas of the woman's legs, hips, and lower back. She must have felt something in those areas, because Doc and the young lady had the following exchange:

"Alicia, how long have you been having knee pain?" Doc asked.

"Wow! You can see that?! Wow!" Alicia was shocked. Then, she continued, "I've been having knee pain for about three months now. The pain is more frequent lately, but it used to be an occasional pain."

Doc swiped a few other areas on the front and back of the knee. Then, she asked, "Is it a fair assumption to say that your knee sometimes goes out when you are going up or down stairs?" Doc asked.

Amazed, and in disbelief, Alicia said, "Yes! I lost my balance just before this presentation. I was coming up the steps to the lodge." Alicia turned her body to look at Doc when she asked, "How could you tell that?" she asked.

"I was able to detect that because I can see that the joints of your knee do not line up correctly and also because of the tone in the muscles surrounding the knee. Alicia, tell me about your menstrual cycles. Your back also tells me you may have issues with your menstrual cycles. Before you answer, let me explain. What I mean by issues is the following: Is your cycle irregular or regular but is extremely heavy in flow. Do you have very bad cramps and/or pain down your legs? Does any of that apply to you?" Doc paused because she saw Alicia wipe tears. She looked around to find her assistant, but he was already walking towards her with Kleenex. "Why are you crying," she asked while handing her the tissue.

"Because I can't believe you are hitting my issues right on the head. I have been having horrible periods for years since high school. I just started my cycle today, and I am cramping so badly. Can you adjust my ovaries?" The crowd laughed.

Doc did, too, and then answered, "Yes."

Stunned, the young lady asked, "Are you serious? Please, do not play with my emotions."

Doc responded, "In essence, yes. The adjustment will indirectly affect the ovaries. May I have your permission to adjust you?"

"Absolutely!" Alicia exclaimed. She eagerly turned over and laid face down.

Doc pulled out a hand held tool that looked like a big syringe. I thought she was getting ready to give her a shot, but the tip of the tool was blunt tipped and spring loaded. When Doc squeezed the handle, you could hear a single click. It sounded like Doc was stapling the lady back together.

Several clicks later, Alicia expressed her astonishment. "Oh, my god! I can feel the cramps going away!" Alicia shrieked from lying face down on the table. After Doc finished adjusting her lower back, Alicia got up from the table with tears streaming down her face. She faced the audience and said, "I know you see tears coming down my face. If you've never been adjusted before, I want you to know my tears are not those of pain, but the absence of pain. What she did with that clicker is nothing short of amazing. Thank you, Doc! You will definitely see me in your office. May I hug you?" Alicia moved in for a hug although Doc had not answer her yet. Even if Doc wanted to avoid contact, Alicia was too quick.

Doc smiled then said, "That's wonderful! You are welcome. But before you run off, can I finish my demonstration?"

"Of course you can!" Alicia happily laid back down on the table. When Doc finished assessing her, Doc had uncovered more about Alicia. Alicia was constipated, suffering from eczema, asthma, recurring headaches, and recurring sore throats.

Amazed and curious as to what my body would say, I wanted to be the next volunteer, but Doc did not have time for a second volunteer. That was okay. I had plans of definitely being in her office soon.

What I had just seen today had been mind blowing. I mean, why am I just now finding out about chiropractic? And, why don't more people know about its benefits?

Chapter 19: Kelly

"Ladies, do you have plans for this down time we have before the dinner tonight?" I asked. Nina and I had made plans to hang out in the hot tub with some wine just to relax.

Sharon answered first. "Not exactly. What did you have in mind?"

"Nina and I are going to chill by the pool or Jacuzzi with some wine. Would you like to join us?" I replied.

The ladies paused to think about it. Sharon spoke first again, "I don't mind putting my bathing suit on for a minute." Then, looking around at the others, she asked, "Who all brought one?" Everyone raised their hands.

Decisively, I said. "Well, let's all meet at the indoor pool in twenty minutes." In agreeance, we all went different ways to our room. Nina and I walked together, in silence. As best friends, we can enjoy each other's company in silence just as well as in conversation. However, our silence was short lived. Marcus appeared in front of us with a female neither of us recognized.

"Nina, baby!" Marcus called as he flashed his charming smile. "I want to introduce you to my sister, Myla." He covered that small distance between us very quickly. I tried, with very little effort, to not appear exasperated. Since I was standing on Nina's right, Marcus stepped to her left, and put his arm around her waist. Nina began to side step, but Marcus tightened his grip a little, and kissed her on the cheek. "Myla, this is my baby, Nina, I was telling you about. She is my heart."

"Bullshit," I coughed. Myla blinked, but never acknowledged me. Interesting. Marcus, too, seemed unbothered by me.

"Hello, Nina. It's a pleasure to meet you," Myla said. She smiled warmly and extended her right hand for a handshake. Ignoring the outstretched hand, Nina returned her greeting with a polite nod and a smile. Myla awkwardly retracted her hand and placed it by her side. "I look forward to getting to know you. I'm sure I'll see more of you."

Before Nina could respond, Marcus spoke, "You will definitely see more of her." He turned to Nina. He stood squarely in front of her, blocking her view of his sister. "He looked into her eyes, and held her gaze for a moment. Then, he placed his forehead against hers while placing his hands on her shoulders. Intently, I watched his every move. If you blinked, you would have missed Nina's attempt to move away from his contact. Marcus had a nice grip on her shoulders. "I will see you later, love," he said, and kisses her lips. Nina bit down on his lip, and held on to it until he cried out. "Damn! What was that for?

I snickered.

Nina side stepped him, and stood in front of Myla. Calmly, she said, "Myla, it is unfortunate that we had to meet under such circumstances. Marcus and I are not a couple. He is full of shit." Nina turned to Marcus who was nursing his lip. "I want you to stop bothering me. I do not want you." Nina looked at me and gave me the cue to leave. Before she walked past Myla, she paused beside her, and said one last thing to her, "The pleasure of meeting you was all Marcus'. Have a good evening."

I looped my arm through Nina's, and we walked away. Once we were out of earshot of Marcus and his sister, I asked her if she was ok. Although she said yes, I knew better. She had given too many non-refundable years of her life to that relationship. Sometimes, we can be foolish like that. We walked the rest of the way in silence.

Inside our room, the silence continued until my cell phone beeped. I had left my phone in the room to charge while we were in the seminars. I had fifteen missed text messages and four missed calls. I had text messages from my cousin, Erica, and my guy friends.

Erica wanted to know if I was free tonight because she he was going to Reggae on the Roof. She knows I have been on a mission to get there since they opened last month. Each time I have made plans to go to the club, something has come up. Tonight would be no different. I was hundreds of miles away on this retreat.

Several text messages were from Mark and Christian, two guys I was dating. I met Mark one day while at the gym. He had been on the stair master next to the one I was attempting to use. I was new to that gym location, and I could not figure out how to work the machine. This machine was drastically different from the one I use at a different location…whenever I went. Ok, actually, that was my first time at the gym in a very long time. I had decided the night before that I was going to exercise and get healthier. Well, I am still working on that.

Mark was very pleasant and patient with me. It did not hurt that he was very handsome. Ten minutes later, I finally had the hang of it, and Mark had finished his workout.

"My name is Mark. Enjoy the rest of your workout!" He smiled as he left. We saw each other several different times at the gym before we exchanged numbers.

Christian was a co-worker who was trying to become more than that. I was not into office romances. I prefer to not to shit where I eat. Christian could not care less. He had his sights set on me, and there was nothing standing between him and me. He began to call and text regularly, which I enjoyed getting. I had begun to anticipate them. His text messages were quite entertaining and VERY stimulating.

As I held the phone in my head, I received another text that had a gif attached to it that read "Thinking of you." I replied quickly, and then walked over to my suitcase. I needed to get my swim suit on. Nina had already changed and was pulling her sweat pants up over her hips.

"Come on chick!" she said. Upon her urging, I went into the bathroom to quickly wash up and dress. I emerged ready to leave.

Nina and I arrived at the pool at the same time as Sharon and Lisa. Jennifer was already at the pool, standing next to the Jacuzzi. She waved us over when she saw us walk in through the door. "Hey, Ladies!" she greeted.

"Hey!" I answered, and waved back. "Were we all moving that slowly that you were able to beat us to the pool?" Jennifer simply shrugged her shoulders in response.

"They have a wet bar here. Let's get a drink and relax," suggested Sharon. She turned to Jennifer and asked, "What would you like to drink? I'll bring it to you."

"Thanks, Sharon. I will take a witch's brew," she answered. Sharon had not been expected such a drink, and her face expressed it. Yet, without any saying anything, she turned on her heels, and began the short walk over to the wet bar. Nina, Lisa, and I followed behind her. As we left, I saw Jennifer place her crutches beside the Jacuzzi and climb in. There was no one at the Wet Bar when we arrived. So, it took the bar tender no time to prepare our drinks. It took an even shorter amount of time to return to Jennifer.

When we were back at the Jacuzzi, everyone climbed in; that is, everyone except Lisa. She stood off to the side of the steps leading into the Jacuzzi while the rest of us became submerged beneath the water.

"Why aren't you getting in, Lisa?" I asked. Just like everyone else, she was dressed for the pool, but did not join us.

She smiled and answered, "No thank you." Her response raised a few eyebrows. We couldn't imagine what would keep her from getting in. There was plenty of room.

I pressed a bit. "Why not? It feels really good." Playfully, I was trying to entice her to change her mind.

"Yeast infection," she said just as calmly.

The ladies and I all shirked away from her general direction, and said in unison, "Yeast infection?" Simultaneously, I think we had arrived at the same thought: She has a yeast infection, and Sharon's response shared that sentiment.

"I'm sorry to hear that you have a yeast infection," Sharon said sincerely.

Laughing at us, Lisa replied, "I did not say I have a yeast infection. I only said 'yeast infection'. The reason I'm not getting into the Jacuzzi with you is because one of you could have a yeast infection. The Jacuzzi is a cesspool. I do not want your vagina juices intermingling near my vagina."

It did not take long for the rest of us to process what Lisa just told us. In fact, we all screeched "Eww" and jumped out of the Jacuzzi. Interestingly enough, Jennifer beat everyone else out of the Jacuzzi.

In utter disbelief, I turned to Jennifer, and said, "How did you get out of there so quickly?! You have one leg less than the rest of us, yet you beat all of us out of the water. Un-believable." I just shook my head while everyone else burst into laughter, which drew attention in our direction.

Shrugging her shoulder, Jennifer answered, "I can't help that you all are slow as molasses." Then, she smiled.

Redirecting the conversation back to Lisa, Sharon said, "I'm glad you shared that information. I do not need any infections near that opening which brings me to my next point. My husband and I are expecting."

We all smiled and congratulated her simultaneously. There is so much joy in hearing that a baby is on its way.

"Thank you, ladies! We are so excited and nervous. This is our second pregnancy. Our first pregnancy did not make it full term, sadly. It was rough trying to heal from the loss. I cried all the time for weeks. Then, I became angry with God. I would yell at him, 'How could you do this to me? How could you be so cruel by letting me become pregnant, and then taking all my hopes and dreams and snatching it all away from me. Then, I became angry and jealous of women who were able to bear healthy children. It was so rough for my husband and me for a long while. One day, after having become patients of doc, and having attending some of her weekly workshops, we decided to try again. During the workshops, we had learned that misalignments in the back could increase the chances of miscarriages. One night, we sat down and had a heart-to-heart conversation about trying again. It was not an easy conversation to have, but I'm happy we did."

Instead of sitting in the Jacuzzi, we were now sitting around the edge of the Jacuzzi. Lisa was still standing.

'Wow! That is fascinating', I thought to myself. I had no idea so many conditions could be associated with the health of the spine. Curious about adjustments while pregnant, I asked, "Will you continue to get treatment while you are pregnant? Is that even possible?"

Sharon turned towards me, and answered, "Yes. According Doc, and some literature I have been reading, it will help my body adopt to the stresses of pregnancy and prepare my body and the baby for delivery."

I do not have a poker face, whatsoever. So, I know my face expressed every bit of my amazement. I had never really given much thought to how stressed the body becomes during pregnancy. Aside from getting stretch marks, it never occurred to me that the spine would undergo any stress from the growth of the baby. Chiropractic is such a hidden jewel. "That's so amazing, Sharon. I had no idea that pregnant women could get adjusted."

"Well," Sharon began, "I am not an expert on this by any means. Why don't you ask Doc more about it? I'm sure she will explain it much better than I ever could."

"Perhaps, I will." I said. Just then, I felt a hand on my shoulder. When I looked over my shoulder, I saw Stephen standing next to me. He was alone.

"Hey, ladies!" he greeted us. "If you all don't mind, I want to take Kelly away from you for a little while." Although that sexy smile never left his face, there was a slight twitch in his neck in response to the looks that were passed between us ladies. He could tell we had just had a whole conversation in that split second, but he did not know what was said. He could only guess.

Sharon winked, "By all means, take her! She will not be missed for a while." Then, she gave me a little nudge as I stood up.

Feigning disgust, I clutched my imaginary pearls, and said, "Well, I've never! I know when I'm not wanted." I gave a small smile in Nina's direction. She gave me a nod, and mouthed, "get 'em girl." Trying not to blush too much, I smiled at Stephen and reached for his outstretched hand. As we walked away, I could hear the cat whistles from the ladies. All I could do was laugh.

Stephen took me to the other side of the pool, near the entrance to the locker rooms. We stopped just at the entrance of the women's locker room. He gave me an admiring look, from head to flip flop clad toes, and said in a sultry voice, "As much as I am enjoying seeing you in your swim wear, I want you to be comfortable." He nodded his towards the locker room door, and said, "Go get dressed, and I will meet you in the lobby."

Relieved and pleased by his consideration, I obliged, and entered the locker room. I quickly slipped my swimsuit off, rinsed it in the sink, and threw it into the spinner to squeeze the water out of it. Then, I oiled my body, and put on my street clothes. Before I stepped out of the locker room, I put some lip gloss on and blew myself a kiss. Satisfied with my appearance, I exited the locker room.

Stephen was standing with his back to me. He had been watching a commercial for zip lining at a nearby winery, and did not immediately notice I was standing next to him. So, I called out to him, "Stephen", while gently placing my hand on his shoulder. At the sound of my voice, or the warmth of my touch, he turned to me and gave me the most beautiful smile. He placed his hand in the small of my back and began directing me towards a love seat on the other side of the reception desk.

"So, what part of town are you from," he asked.

"I live in midtown, near the universities. Where do you live?" I countered, and took a seat. The love seat was very cozy, to say the least. As much as I was trying to avoid body contact, it was inevitable. He let his leg rest comfortably against mine.

"I live in the Heights, out west. Perhaps, one day you will grace my home with your presence?" He paused, shifted his body towards me more, and placed his arm along the back of the love seat. What cologne was he wearing? It was intoxicating and alluring. "Tell me. What do you enjoy doing," he said.

"Well", I began, "I enjoy doing a lot of things; from watching musicals to shooting pool and throwing darts." Just as I was getting ready to share more, he interrupted.

"Musicals?! So, let me guess. You have season passes to the Muny?" he said as he shook his head and chuckled.

I was not surprised by his reaction at all. Every time I tell guys I enjoy musicals, they typically respond like this. However, I was not prepared for what Stephen would soon reveal.

"What is your favorite musical?" he asked.

"Grease. I love Grease," I said.

Without warning, he sang, "Grease lightening! Goooo, grease lightening!" He even did the choreography! I was shocked and tickled!

"Where did THAT come from? Are you a closet fan of Grease?" I asked.

He laughed, "I am a closet fan of musicals. Now, I don't have any season passes to the Muny, but I occasionally enjoy a musical at the park. If you don't have any objections, I would love to accompany you to one next summer."

As our conversation continued, I became aware of my new position on the love seat. I had closed the slight gap that once existed between us. Now, my knee was angled towards him, and resting comfortably against his, as if drawn to him like a magnet. I also noticed that he was leaning in as well. I felt myself staring at his thick, sexy lips. Forcing myself not to stare, I averted my attention to the television screen mounted on the lobby wall. Then, I remembered to ask him the same question he had asked me, "So, tell me. What do you enjoy doing?"

He answered, "I love long walks on the beach, and watching the sun set." Then, he laughed at his own joke. "But for real, I enjoy swimming laps at the pool, playing basketball, shooting pool, and throwing darts. Do you swim?" I gave him a look that said, 'Seriously?' He chuckled, and said, "What? You don't want to mess up your hair?"

Shrugging my shoulders, I replied, "Laugh all you want. And, yes, that is one of the reasons. Ok, a major reason. I invest too much into my hair and it takes too much time to do my hair. So, no, I do not get in the pool. Besides, I never learned to swim." I said matter-of-factly.

Still laughing, he said, "Now THAT should be the reason why you don't get in the pool; not the fact that you don't want to mess up your hair." Then, he shook his head. "Whew, my sister!" Once his laughter subsided, he had a thoughtful look on his face.

"What is that look for?" I asked.

"I was just wondering if you would change your mind about getting in the pool if I was in the pool. I may not be able to resolve the issue with your hair, but I can definitely resolve the latter issue of not knowing how to swim. I would love to teach you if you will let me," he said.

I cocked my head to the side, and looked at him. The look on his face was serious. He really wants to teach me how to swim. Still thinking about my hair, I answered, "We'll see." He smiled sweetly before asking me another question.

"Why do you eat?" he asked.

I was so confused. Where did that question come from? What does he mean 'why do I eat'? Why would he ask me that question? I answered, "Doesn't everyone eat for the same reason; because they are hungry? Why do you ask?"

"I wanted to see what your perspective was on food. Actually, everyone does not eat for the same reason. Some people eat under stress. Some eat because they are hungry. Then, there are people such as myself, who eat to live. I eat on purpose."

I have never heard of such a concept. Interesting. "What does that mean," I asked.

"What I mean by that is, I eat with the intent of giving my body energy and strengths to enjoy life. I try to make sure my meals always have the correct proportion of protein, carbohydrates, and healthy fats. Not by any means am I perfect at doing this, but I do my best," he answered.

Stephen probably did not mean anything by his question. Yet, I felt like he was attacking me. I'm not sure why exactly. As if sensing the change in my mood, Stephen changed the subject. "I apologize if I have offended you. That was not my intent. Please forgive me."

He sounded so sincere. His voice was gentle. "I appreciate the apology."

"What's your favorite movie?" he asked.

"A Family That Preys" I answered without pause. By the look on his face, I could tell he was not familiar with the movie. "Have you never heard of the movie before?" Talking about the movie changed my mood. My face was less pinched, and my shoulders had relaxed.

"I think I may have heard of that movie, but I do not fully recall it. Who is in it?" Sensing my mood change, his body began to reflect it. He had shifted away from me when he felt like he had offended me. But, since I was relaxed again, I noticed that he had shifted his body in my direction. His right knee was now resting on my left knee and he had placed his arm along the back of the loveseat.

Extremely aware of his presence, I found it difficult to focus on my answer to the question. The cologne he wore was intoxicating to my senses. His eyes were so big, bright, and playful. When he smiled, his dimple deepened in his right cheek. His teeth were so straight and white. I wondered how often he whitened his teeth.

Just then, his cell phone rang. His ringtone was that of a woodpecker. I shot him the side eye, to which he laughed as he pulled his phone out of his pocket. Answering the question I had not verbalized, he said, "I wanted a ringtone no one else had."

"Nailed it," I said.

"I'm surprised to be getting a call. I have not had much service out here during this retreat." He said as he looked down at the screen of the phone. Whose ever name he read definitely changed his mood. Then, he excused himself to take the call. While he was taking the call, the ladies exited the locker room. They spotted Stephen over by the big bay window overlooking the lake before they looked around the room and saw me sitting on the loveseat. When they did see me, they all walked over to me with mischievous grins on their faces. Nina was the first to speak.

"How is it going out here," she asked.

Trying my hardest not blush, I said, "It's going fine. We were having a pretty good conversation. Just before you all came out, his phone rang and he walked away to take the call. Where are you all heading?"

"It is about that time we should get ready for dinner." Lisa said. She looked over her should at Stephen, who seemed to be finishing up his call, and then back at me. "Do you want us to wait for you, or will you have Stephen escort you to the room?" Lisa, who was clearly rooting for a love connection between us, hoped for the latter.

Blushing, still, I answered, "You all go ahead. I will wait for him." Peering over her shoulder, I could see he was heading our way.

Smiling and then winking, Nina said, "Well, I will see you back at the room."

The other ladies smiled and waved as they walked towards the front entrance. As they exited, Stephen came to the right side of the loveseat, and leaned on his elbows on the armrest next to me. His face was only inches away from the side of my face. I could smell the spearmint scented gum in his mouth. I turned to meet his gaze. He smiled, and leaned in for a kiss. Of course I did not turn it down. I had been daydreaming about kissing his sexy lips all day, trying to imagine if they were as soft as they looked. I leaned in and accepted the kiss. Yes!!! Those juicy lips were as soft as they looked. My, my, my!!! That kiss made me feel tingly all over. Whew!

"Since it is about that time for us to get ready for dinner, let me walk you to your room, if that is ok with you," he said. His eyes were now hooded by his eyelids, and his voice had deepened; as if his voice could get any sexier.

Softly, I said, "Of course it is." My heart was racing. I wanted more contact, but I had to stay cool. I did not want to appear thirsty.

Chapter 20: Stephen

After I had walked Kelly to her room, I could not help but grin all the way to my room. The more I spoke to Kelly and discovered who she is, the more intrigued I became. Her energy was awesome. Man, I really like her! I just hope she feels the same about me.

As I reached the entrance to my cabin, my phone vibrated. It was a text message from my best friend, Cheyenne. She was wondering if I was enjoying myself at the retreat. I stopped short of opening the door, and sat down on the edge of the wooden bench to the right of the big flower pot. I wanted to quickly respond to Cheyenne. I told her the retreat was going better than I had expected and that I was enjoying myself. Then, she asked about Sean and Lisa. She had met them through me. . Although she is not that close to them, she is quite fond of them. I told her they were doing great. Then, I told her about the dinner tonight; that I needed to get dressed; and that I will call her when I get back to the Lou. She responded one last time with "Ok."

I removed my room key from my pant pocket and unlocked the door. The room was filled with the sounds of jazz blaring from Sean's Bluetooth wireless speaker, which was connected to his iPod. Pandora was pulled up and deejaying from the Smooth Jazz station. As I placed my key on the night stand between the beds, a jazzy rendition of "Just My Imagination" began to play. When I looked up, Sean was coming out of the bathroom with shaving cream on his face.

"What time did you get back?" I asked. While I was with Kelly, I never paid any attention to the fellas leaving the rec center. I guess I was so preoccupied with Kelly that I failed to pay attention to my surroundings. That's not typical of me. He

"I have been here for about ten or fifteen minutes," he answered while rummaging through his carry-on until he had found the after shave he was seeking. Then, he turned on his heels and headed back into the bathroom.

Just before he disappeared into the bathroom, I asked and nodded towards the bathroom, "How long will you be?"

He shrugged, "Not much longer. Fifteen minutes maybe?" he answered, and closed the door.

I decided to use that fifteen minutes to get my clothes ready. From my dress bag, I removed my coal gray, tailored Ralph Lauren slacks, white French cuff shirt, Royal blue blazer, and silver round cuff links. Then, I laid my Armani wrist watch on the bed.

As a fan. As a fan of secret agent type movies like 007, owning an Armani watch was the closest I could get to that lifestyle since Armani is inspired by spies.

Almost to the minute, fifteen minutes later, Sean emerged from the bathroom in his bath robe with a lot of steam in his wake. He walked over to his suit hanging in the open closet. "Did you leave any hot water for me" I joked.

"About ten ounces which is more than enough for you," he answered without missing a beat.

"I will give the bathroom a minute to air out." Just then, my phone vibrated. This time, it was my brother calling. "Hello?" I answered. My brother sounded slightly alarming. "What's up, Mike?" He told me nothing, at first. Then, he said he was looking for mama. She was supposed to be meeting him at a church function that started a half hour ago. He said he has been calling her house phone and cell phone, but was not getting an answer. "Well, I will call and see if I can catch her. Call Aunt Mary to see if she is with her." He agreed, and hung up the phone.

"Is everything ok?" Sean asked after overhearing my end of the conversation.

"Yeah. My brother is trying to find my mother. They were supposed to meet up a half hour ago, and she has not shown up yet." I said, "She probably lost tract of time in a store. She is good for doing that." I called my mom's phone as promised. No answer. Unbothered, I tossed the phone onto the bed as I headed into the bathroom. Turning away as the phone left my hand, I did not notice that it had bounced off of the bed, and onto the floor on the other side of the bed near the wall.

About twenty minutes later, I came out of the bathroom. Sean was not in the room, but I could tell he had not gone far. Smooth jazz was still belting from the iPod. This time, "Cruising" was playing. I checked the digital clock next to the iPod. Dinner would be starting in less than a half hour. It took me another ten minutes to dress. Sean walked in just as I slid my feet into my shoes.

"Are you ready?" he asked as he walked over to the ipod. He powered down the iPod and placed it into its case.

I stood up, popped my collar, and said, "Show you right! I was born ready."

"Really?" Sean sarcastically responded. "You sound like an old man when you say that."

"Oh, yeah? Well, how about this one? *Everything is copasetic.*" I said mockingly.

With more sarcasm, "Oh, yes! That's much better! Now, you sound like my grandmother." He shook his head, and we both laughed. "Come on, man. Let's get to the banquet center. I am hungry and ready to see my wife."

I grabbed my watch off of the bed and followed Sean out of the door. As he walked past the light switch at the entrance of the cabin, he flipped the switch to off. Our other cabin mates weren't there. Anthony had left earlier for the banquet. Sean told me he had left while I was in the shower. Although Sean said he has seen Marcus a couple of times, I have yet to meet him.

The banquet center was located in one of the newer buildings on the camp grounds. It was about a five minute walk up the road from the main lodge, which was already a three to five minute walk from our cabin. It was a good thing my shoes were comfortable. I can only imagine the discomfort of walking over this gravel from our cabin.

"When was the last time you've heard from Christine?" Sean asked, breaking my thoughts about Kelly.

"She text me the other day, pleading for me to tell her the truth." I answered.

"Tell her the truth about what?" Sean asked. I had only told Sean that Christine and I had called it quits. I had not given much details because we have not had time to sit down and catch up on things.

"For a little over a year now, our relationship has been strained. You know she always loved the money I was bringing in. And, she really loved the money that I started bringing in with the new promotion. However, she was not too fond of the increased amount of time that I was being required to put in at the office. To top it off, for the last few months, our sex life has been very uneventful. To be more precise, our sex life has been non-existent." I answered. As I spoke, I realized that this was the first time I have spoken about what was going on with me.

"Why is your sex life practically non-existent?" Sean inquired.

I took a deep breath before starting, but kept my voice low. There were now people a few paces ahead of us walking toward the banquet center. "After the car accident last year, it has been a struggle to get back to my pre-accident self. I still have persistent pain in my back. Therapy gives me occasional relief but not complete relief. Don't get me wrong. I have made significant progress because of therapy, but I feel like I need a little bit more of something else for relief."

"Steph, that is to be expected, I would think, considering how terrible that wreck was," he said.

"I get that, but there are other things I have noticed in the last several months. Look man, what I have to say next is far from easy to say, but it is really bothering me." I began.

"Uh, do I want to know?" he interrupted me.

"Most likely not, but I need someone to tell this to, and you are my boy. I trust you. Besides, I do not know who else to speak to about this. The reason our sex life has been non-existent is because I can't...you know..." I said.

"You can't what?" he probed.

I sighed. "I can't get an erection." Sean became quiet for a few moments. "If I am lucky enough to get one, it does not last like it used to. So, Christine took it as an indication of me cheating on her. She is under the impression that my long days at work are not work related. She thinks I am seeing someone else as to why I am not sexually attracted to her anymore. At first, work was the reason for the long days. Then, it became my escape. I used it to avoid coming home to her." I said as we continued walking down the well-lit gravel road.

"Why didn't you just tell her about your 'issue'?" Sean asked.

"After the accident, she changed. I met a different side of Christine when I became dependent on her. I could not drive to therapy. So, she had to change her schedule to accommodate, and she did not like it. She would ask me where my family was. Why weren't they around to help? They were there. My mom and brother came by the house while she was at work or simply out and about. When she was home, she begrudgingly helped me move around the house. It was obvious that she was agitated that she had to help me. The only thing she seemed to enjoy doing was bringing me my laptop for me to do work. She knew that was going to keep the money rolling in. I have been asked by my brother do I have any regrets about the way things have happened, from the day of the accident and on. I told him, no. The accident allowed me to see who really cared about me."

"That's messed up. I didn't know you were dealing with all of that. Why did you keep all of this to yourself?" Sean asked.

"Man, you know I am not a whiner. I was going to press through. Besides, you have your own life to live." We were now a few hundred feet from the banquet center. I stopped to face Sean, "Look, I said all of that to say this, I need a solution for my…" I paused until some people walked pass to enter the building. Then, I whispered 'issue'. "I really like Kelly, and I do not want *that* to be a deal breaker."

"As you know, I am not a doctor. However, I would suggest that you speak to Doc before the end of the weekend. Ask her if she has any suggestions for you, or if she can steer you towards the right people." Sean answered. Sean was getting ready to say something else, when I suddenly interrupted him.

"Hold that thought. I have to go to the bathroom. That's another thing I have to deal with since the accident. I'll find you once you get inside." I said, and headed inside. I had been holding my pee during the short walk down here. Now, I had to go badly. I didn't even wait to hold the door open for Stephen. I'm sure he understood.

Chapter 21: Kelly

I stood on the other side of the door to my room, and listened to Stephen walk down the hall. All I could do was blush girlishly. I had not been standing there for more than a minute when Nina walked out of the bathroom. Nina had obviously just finished her makeup. Her face was flawless. She has serious skills when it comes to makeup.

"Hey, Kelly! Finally, made it to the room, I see." She smiled at me; and immediately, I began smiling from ear to ear.

"Whoa! As much as I would love to think that smile was for me, I surely know better. That smile was because of Mr. Wonderful," she said. Like a little school girl, I giggled. "And she giggles!" she continued to tease.

Blushing, all I could muster was, "Whatever," and walked into the bathroom. I stood in front of the mirror and smiled at myself. Then, my smile faded and was replaced with a look of disappointment. I walked over to the toilet, sat down, and peed. When I finished, I wiped myself and peered down at the tissue. Just as I thought. My cycle was starting. *Ain't this some shit! I can't catch a break!* My cycle comes when it wants to and stays as long as it wants to. *I am so sick of this!* While I continued sitting, I just hung my head. I had just gotten off my period at the end of last week. That period had lasted ten days. I guess I had been too quiet for too long in the bathroom, because Nina began knocking on the door.

"Did you fall in?" she joking asked.

Sullenly, I responded, "Nah, I didn't."

Noting the change in my voice, Nina asked, "Are you alright? What's wrong, boo?"

"Nothing." I lied. "Will you do me a favor? Will you look in my carry-on and bring me a sani-cup? It is in a Ziploc bag."

There was a pause before Nina said anything. Then, she said, "Um, what is a sani-cup?"

Not wanting to explain through the door, I answered, "I have a Ziploc bag with small rubber cups in them. They are almost the size of a mouthwash cup."

"Soooo, we are going to pretend that I did not just ask you what is a sani-cup? Ok. That's fine. I'll go get your rubber mouthwash cups anyway." Nina said before walking away from the door. About a minute or so later, she returned to the door. "Is the door locked?"

"No, come in." Yep, I was still sitting on the toilet. Nina walked over to me, handed me the bag, grabbed her hair brush off of the vanity, and walked out.

The sani-cup was about the only 'plus' to my irregular cycles, if ever there was such a thing. This allows me to not have to change a napkin or tampon regularly. It is easy to use, and it is supposed to be healthier than the other options. I don't know how true that is, but I like it. I inserted it and continued on with what I needed to do to get ready for the evening.

It took me thirty minutes to shower, and oil my body. I was wearing a hairstyle that required no maintenance; a protective hairstyle. Since I was planning to get Nina to do my makeup, all I did was apply some moisturizer.

Donned in my robe, I walked out of the bathroom. Nina was standing by the window trying to find a spot for cellular reception. Somewhat exasperated, Nina put her arm down, cell phone in hand. "When they say come here to retreat, they mean it literally. I have struggled to figure out where in this lodge I can get consistent enough reception. Yet, somehow, Marcus keeps getting through." She looked up at me. "What's wrong, Kelly? Why the sudden mood swing? Talk to me while I get the makeup together." She began gathering everything, and I sat in the chair at the desk in the room.

"I'm often told to stop whining; to suck it up whenever I talk about how bad my periods have gotten. It seems they are always present and I don't get a break. They are irregular. I never know when it is coming. I have to always keep sani-cups and a party-liner with me. When they do come, I get terrible cramps, back pain, and pain in my thighs. While I'm mentioning it, let me take some powder to try to get ahead of my pain." I reached over to the foot of my bed, which was across from the desk, and grabbed my little makeup bag. My powder was inside, just next to my small mirror. I opened the packet. Using my index finger, I put the power on my tongue and let it dissolve.

Nina now had all of the makeup and tools she needed. She tilted the lamp shade on the desk to direct the light on to my face. Because I had already applied moisturizer, she began with foundation. Since we are the same complexion, she was able to use her foundation. Next, she applied a primer to my eyelids followed by shades of gold and brown eyeshadows. She gave my eyes the dramatic look. She also put highlights on my cheekbones. Fifteen minutes later, I was looking like a supermodel. After seeing myself in the mirror, my mood simply could not stay in the dumps. I looked radiantly. Also, I couldn't wait for Stephen to see me.

I quickly changed into my gown, and ran my fingers through my hair. I stood in front of the mirror, and admired myself. I looked breathtakingly beautiful, even if I had to say so myself. I continued standing there because I just could not stop looking at myself.

"Thank you, Nina." I said, finally turning away from the mirror. When I looked over at Nina, she was putting her earrings in her ear.

"You are so welcome." She put her bracelet on and turned to me. "Did you think I forgot about your mood swing? What was that all about and what is a sani-cup?"

Shifting my focus from my appearance in the mirror to what Nina was asking, my facial expression exposed my exasperation. I sighed and explained to her that a sani-cup is a rubber cup that you insert inside the vagina during your cycle. First, you have to pinch or sort of fold the cup tight. Then, you push it up inside the vagina. Once it is all the way in, you let go and the cup pops open to seal the opening and collect the flow. Afterwards, I explained to her how my menstrual cycle practically controls my life.

"Um Kelly, you are miserable! You are not living life. You are just surviving. I know firsthand. Although I went to Doc for my jaw pain, she uncovered a lot of other issues with my body that I did not think was related to or even treated with chiropractic care. One of the things she asked me about was my periods because of something that showed up during the examination. It blew my mind. Weeks into my treatment, I noticed my period was lighter and a day shorter than usual."

"Really?" Now that she is mentioning it, I never really asked what she was getting out of going to the chiropractor. As she continued, I reached for the Kleenex that was on the desk next to the lamp.

"Yes. I experienced all of those things you mentioned, as well as those that were mentioned by the lady who had volunteered during the presentation; including the pain down my thigh when my cycle started, back pain, headaches, and mood swings; the works. When Sharon told me about Doc, she just happened to have mentioned that her cycles were better than they have ever been before she started getting adjusted. When Sharon told me that tidbit, she had no clue what I was dealing with regarding my menstrual cycles. All she knew was that my jaw was giving me the blues. Little did she know, she had given me that extra encouragement I needed to go see Doc. I will tell you this: I'm so very glad I did."

Nina continued, "The week I had my first appointment also happened to be the same week I was having a cycle. I was six days in with a very heavy flow. After my first adjustment, I noticed a decrease in the volume of flow that night. The next day or two I was off. I continued getting adjustments. Before long, my cycle was regular. Now, I have one cycle every 29 days with minimal cramping, or none at all, and it only lasts for 5 days tops. Another thing I noticed was that my Eczema cleared up a lot! I don't know if this is the case with everyone, but by the time Doc finished my adjustment, my skin was irritated as much. Within a few adjustments, the rash on my elbow had cleared up. Honey, I wasn't living life before. Now, I am loving life. I feel so much better, and I got my sexy back. Kelly, you need to see Doc this week. You will benefit in some way from it."

Surprisingly, her story made me feel more at ease. It never occurred to me that she was having any of those issues she was dealing with. My mom always say, 'You never know what people are going through. They may be all happy in public, but are crying behind closed doors.' After a moment of thought, I turned to Nina, "I will call her office on Monday."

"Great! Now let's finish getting dressed," Nina said. Then, she looked in my face and said, "I'm surely glad I used waterproof mascara!"

I threw my balled up tissue paper at her, and said, "Whatever."

"I'm just saying, the makeup made your ugly cry face cute", she laughed.

Chapter 22:   Lisa

"Aye, Papi", I said to my husband when he walked into the banquet hall. I love seeing my man dressed in a suit. He is so sexy to me, still, three years later. I am so in love with him.

"Hey, Mamacita," he said before kissing me on my lips. "You look stunning!"

"Thank you! You are making me blush," I said while playfully swatting at him. "Are you ready for this three course meal and some music?"

"Absolutely. Where are we sitting?" he said.

I pointed him to the table I had picked out for the seven of us to sit together. As we headed to the table, Stephen joined us. He had been in the men's room. He looked really nice. I could not wait to see Kelly's reaction when she saw him. No sooner had that thought crossed my mind did Kelly and Nina walk in. Kelly wore a coral colored halter gown with a peek-a-boo slit between her breasts. She also wore black, open toe high heels. The heel of the shoe was decorated with studs while the rest of the shoe was a solid black. Nine wore a gold asymmetric gown with a solid black pump that strapped around her ankles. They looked beautiful. Now, I really could not wait to see Stephen's reaction to Kelly. Stephen's back was to Nina and Kelly, but he must have felt their presence, because he turned around just in time to watch Kelly strut to the table.

"Good evening, ladies," Stephen said. Then, focusing his attention on Kelly, he said, "Kelly, you look amazing!"

My husband and Stephen both made their way around the table to pull all of our chairs out. Sean pulled my seat out, and then Nina's, who was standing to my left, before taking his own seat out. On Nina's left, Stephen pulled out Kelly's chair. He grabbed her left hand, kissed it gently, and led her around the chair to help her sit down. Then, he sat down himself. As everyone became comfortable, Sharon and Anthony walked up to the table.

"Good evening, everyone", they said. "May we join you?"

I cocked my head to the right, and asked, "Really?"

They laughed and sat down. Anthony pulled out Sharon's chair before sitting in his own.

There was still one more seat unoccupied at the table. It was for Jennifer, whenever she got here. Just then, she entered the banquet hall. She wore this gorgeous, floor length, all black gown, with a thigh high split on the right. She wore on her foot a shimmering gold pump that strapped around her ankle. I stood up and waved her over to the table. We all watched admiringly as she made her way over to us.

"Ms. Jennifer, you look amazing!" Sean said, as he pulled her chair out for her.
"Thank you, honey!" she said playfully. "Don't you all look darling?!" She said after she was comfortably sitting in her chair.

"Jennifer, you are such a diva! I really love your spunk. I mean, you are so full of life. And, you are wearing that split. I must say, I never would have imagined that a woman with one leg would wear a dress with a split that high," said Kelly. The ladies are moaned, "Really, Kelly?"

Jennifer just laughed, and waved her hand at the table. "Kelly doesn't mean any harm. I am not offended." Then, Jennifer turned to Kelly, "I do not care that I only have one leg. I am going to accent my uniqueness. In fact, my leg is one sexy leg. Did you notice the muscle definition? My leg game is better than a lot women's." Then, she snapped her finger to stress her point. All we could do was laugh. Jennifer was hilarious!

Throughout dinner, we enjoyed good food and good conversations. The conversation even went back to what we saw in the Posturing for Inner Peace presentation. It made us reflect on our very first visit with Doc.

"When I filled out the paperwork, I was like 'Damn! They want to know all of my business.' What really got me was the long questionnaire that asked if you have had any symptoms such as sinus/allergies, constipation, headaches, or rashes. Now, in my head, I was thinking: What does this have to do with my neck or back hurting," Sharon said.

"Right!" Nina said, "The new patient packet is a book. But what about when Doc is examining you? Before you get started you have no idea you are getting ready to through all of these exercises. She has you moving in ways you usually do NOT move because it hurts to do so. It felt like a workout class."

"Oh, and what about when she checked your posture! Did you expect that firm pressure from her little hands? I thought someone else had walked into the room. Nope. It was just her. She is gentle but firm," said Lisa.

"She does give you plenty of warning that she is getting ready to touch you, but I still wasn't ready. She tells you what she is going to do; then she does it," said Sean.

We all joked and laughed some more until we had reached the end of dinner. Doc walked over to the mic where she said a few words to close out the dinner before turning the room over to the DJ.

"Please, enjoy the rest of the night and dance until your feet get sore while DJ Vynil finesse those turntables."

DJ Vynil leaned into the mic, and said, "Really, Doc?" Everyone in the banquet hall erupted into laughter.

Doc cracks me up when she tries to be hip with her lingo. She does not sound hip at all.

The first song the DJ played was "Let's Go Crazy" by Prince. Everyone was ready to dance and burn some calories. Several songs into the night, everyone heard, "It's the Casper Slide Part 2", and the floor filled up quickly. Even Stephen and Sean joined the lines. Then, a slow song played. It was *Permission* by Ro James. Sean pulled me close, and held me tightly. Looking mischievously around the room, as if making sure no one could hear him, he said, "I've been wanting to snatch that dress off of you since I walked through the door."

I replied, "I have been thinking the same thing." I looked around and grabbed his hand. I, then, grinned and said, "Come on. Let's go."

Chapter 23: Stephen

The dance ended close to midnight. After the dance, I walked Kelly to her room. I resisted the urge to kiss her goodnight. Instead, I shook her hand, and walked away.

Back at my room, I showered and changed into my bed clothes. As I placed my clothes into my overnight bag, I checked my pockets for my cellphone. Not feeling it, I began to panic. Where had I left my phone? I tried to think back to the last time I had my phone. At first, I thought it was when I was when I was in the lobby of the rec center. Then, I remembered having had a conversation with my brother while I was in this room before going to the banquet. My phone had to be in this room.

I walked around the main area of the room. It wasn't on the nightstand between the double beds. And, it wasn't on the desk or dresser in the room. Where could it be? I just happened to walk around to the other side of my bed, and there on the floor was my phone. It must have bounced out of the bed when I had thrown it onto the bed.

When I picked up the phone, I saw many missed calls and text messages from my brother. He had even left voicemails. I listened to the first voice. My brother was frantic and crying. I couldn't make out much, but I did hear that mom was in the hospital. My heart began pumping rapidly. What has happened to mom?

I quickly gathered my clothes, and packed my bag. I scribbled a note to Sean on a pad that was on the desk telling him I had to leave for a family emergency and that I will touch bases with him when he gets home. I also thanked him in advance for bringing my bag home. With that, I grabbed my leather jacket, my keys, wallet, and left out of the cabin. I hopped on my motorcycle and headed north.

Chapter 24: Kelly

Not everyone made it to the breakfast the next morning, I noticed. Nina and I were there, and so were Sharon and Anthony. But, Lisa, Stephen, and Sean were missing in action. I wondered where they were.

It was now 11:07 a.m. on Sunday, and people were starting to load up the bus. Nina and I were next in line for the driver to take our bags when Lisa and Sean came up. There were all googly-eyed and cheesing. I can now guess why they did not make it to breakfast. I still had not seen who I was looking for: Stephen.

"Hey, Sean. Good morning. Have you seen Stephen? I wanted to tell him goodbye." I said.

Sean came to stand next to me. "Oh, I'm sorry. Stephen had to leave suddenly in the middle of the night. He had an emergency and needed to hit the road", he answered.

I guess my face showed how I crestfallen I felt because Sean asked, "Hey, what's wrong? Can't you call him? Did you two not exchange numbers?"

Shaking my head, I replied, "No, but it is okay, though." I was disappointed. I had hoped there was more to this weekend than those few shared moments. I really enjoyed his company. And it did not hurt that he was easy on the eyes. I was getting ready to turn and walk away when Sean made a suggestion.

"How about you give me your number? I will send him your number so he can call you. I am sure he would love to have your number, and probably would have gotten it this morning if he had not had to rush off last night", he said.

I typed and saved my number in his cell phone. When I handed the phone back to him, he gave me a hug. Then, Lisa hugged me. "We will be in touch. I look forward to spending time with you all when we get back to St. Louis."

"Me, too." I said.

Nina stepped forward to give Sean and Lisa both a hug, too. We were not able to say our goodbyes to Sharon and Anthony. They had gotten on the road an hour ago.

Nina and I waved one last time to Sean and Lisa, and then boarded the bus. I sat by the window and closed my eyes for the ride home. It was my best attempt to hide my sadness.

December

Chapter 25: Nina

'In eight hundred feet, your destination is on the right,' my GPS said. I was trying to find this Italian restaurant in Frontenac on the corner of Clayton Road and Lindbergh. I have never been to this restaurant, but I have been to the 'brother' restaurant in West County. The correct term to use was probably 'sister' restaurant, but because the names of both restaurants end in 'o', in most foreign languages, that would imply masculinity, I decided to call them brothers. Just my thoughts.

'You have arrived', said my GPS, although I was still on Lindbergh. The entrance into the parking lot was little ways down. So, I had to pass up the restaurant and then double back. Just after I pulled into a parking space, another car pulled up next to me. When I looked over, I saw Ms. Jennifer.

For a seventy something year old woman, she looks fabulous. I could only hope to look as great as her. She has super toned arms. The average person may assume that her toned arms were a result of walking around on crutches. However, that is far from her situation. She spends at least eight hours a week in the gym lifting weights. She said that, although she lifts, her physique comes from a clean diet. Lifting and working out was for toning. For someone with only one leg, that was the best looking leg I have every personally seen. It looked like a leg out of the Grey's Anatomy textbook; the book I saw on Doc's bookshelf at the office.

We both exited our respective cars simultaneously. Despite knowing what her answer would be, I asked her if I could help her. As I expected, she said, 'No, I got it'; and of course, she did.

Once she was completely out of her car and standing next to the closed driver door, I walked up to her and gave her a hug. This was the first time I had seen her since the retreat. As I released her, she inquired about Kelly, Lisa, and Sharon. "Have the others arrived yet?"

It has almost been two months since the retreat. Although we had remained in contact via text messages and phone calls, this would be the first time we are together all at once; somewhat anyway. I told Ms. Jennifer Kelly will not be joining us this evening because she had her new patient orientation at Doc's office this evening.

Together, Ms. Jennifer and I walked up to the entrance of the restaurant. We were moving quite briskly because of the chill in the air. The temperature was forty-two degrees and the wind was biting. I grabbed for the door handle to open the door, but the door swung up. Sean was holding the door open for us.

"Good evening, Ladies," he greeted us. He gave me a hug, and then Ms. Jennifer. "You two look lovely," he said and began helping Ms. Jennifer out of her coat. While he assisted Ms. Jennifer, I walked over to Lisa and greeted her with a hug. When I hugged her close, I could feel a little baby bump.

"Oh my God!" I gasped, and beamed from ear to ear. "The pregnancy is coming along well, yes?!"

"Absolutely! It has been an amazingly smooth ride thus far," she continued to beam. Her pregnancy glow was so beautiful. Just then, the door of the restaurant opened again. It was Sharon and Anthony!

"Hey!" I said. Lisa and I walked over to them, and waited for our turn to hug and greet. Ms. Jennifer was the closest to them. So, they hugged her first. Then, Anthony and Sharon made their way through the rest of us.

The maître'd approached me. "Is your whole party here and ready to be seated?"

I answered, "Yes, we are all here."

"Right this way, please," he said. He sure was a nice looking brother. Dressed in a light purple button up collared shirt with black slacks on, my guess was that he was one of the managers. The servers and bus boys were all wearing all black button up collared shirts and black pants. He led us by the window that had a view of the dimly lit patio. As we took our seats, he placed menus down in front of each seat, and then told us our server will be right with us.

While we waited, Sharon asked about Kelly. I told everyone she was at the new patient orientation at Doc's office tonight.

"Really?!" asked Sean. "Well, isn't that convenient?"

We all looked at him inquisitively, and he chuckled. "Your faces are priceless. Anyway, I said that because that is the same reason why Stephen is not here tonight. He wanted to come so he could see Kelly. Well, apparently, his wish has been granted. He will get to see her after all." We, too, chuckled.

Ever since they met at the retreat, I had always felt they made a cute couple. They look really good together. It was my hope they do connect after the orientation. Kelly was so disappointed when she did not hear from Stephen after the retreat. She really liked him. Now, I cannot wait to talk to her when I get home.

"Since we are due around the same time, we were thinking how cute it would be for our babies to grow up together and have play dates." I heard Lisa say as I came out of my own thoughts. Everyone at the table listened to Sharon and Lisa go on and on about pregnancy for a little while, ever after the server took our order and brought our drinks. Ms. Jennifer eventually decided to change the subject. She was not all that interest in hearing about babies all night.

"So, Nina, what is new in your world?" Ms. Jennifer asked me. "You are looking really good. You look more toned than the last time I saw you. What have you been doing lately?"

I groaned inwardly. I did not want all the attention on me, but everyone was patiently waiting for my reply.

"Well, I have been swimming these days. I am planning to do my first triathlon in a couple of months." I answered.

"A triathlon?!" they all exclaimed.

"Remind me. What are the three events?" Ms. Jennifer asked.

"Swimming, biking, and running. I am only doing an indoor sprint. I am moving for an hour. I will be doing a ten minute swim, twenty minute biking, and then, thirty minutes run, jog on the treadmill," I said.

"Wow! So, you are superwoman?!" Anthony said.

I laughed, "Not at all. I am just challenging myself.

"That is quite some challenge!" Sean said. "Swimming, no less!"

"Swimming was a big challenge for me to overcome. I did not know much about swimming. I have been working with a swim coach."

"Well, good for you, and good luck! Be sure to give us the date so we can come cheer you on from the audience," Sean said. Everyone agreed with him.

"I surely will." I said.

Shortly thereafter, our food arrived. I had ordered the salmon salad with double salmon. It tasted as delicious as it smelled. Very little talking was going on while we ate. We must have all been very hungry.

We all continued the rest of the evening for another hour before we finally began to wrap it. Besides, we could tell that the server was ready for us to leave, too. Just as we had greeted each other, we bid each other farewell.

Until we meet again, friends!

Chapter 26:   Stephen

I was sitting in Doc's waiting room. I was waiting on her new patient official welcome to begin. I had arrived early because I was already in the area. It did not make sense for me to drive all the way home and have to turn right around to come back. Before coming in, I waited in my car for twenty minutes. Then, I came on in.

I had been sitting in the waiting room less than five minutes when my phone rang. It was Sean.

"What's up?" I answered, trying to keep my voice low.

"What are you doing this evening? I forgot to tell you about the dinner with everyone we met at the retreat. You know, Sharon, Nina, Ms. Jennifer and them. Why don't you swing through?" he said.

"I am at Doc's for the Official Welcome she does for new patients. I do not know what time I am getting out of here." I said. Then, Kelly crossed my mind. Will she be there?

Breaking into my thoughts, Sean said, "Yo! Have you called Kelly yet? That has been on my mind all day", he said.

I had been wanting to call her ever since Sean text me the number, but I was nervous about it. I really like Kelly, and I really want to be with her, but I was scared. Although I know I had so much to offer her, I worried about being able to please her. My shit had not been quite up to par for a year. Even though I have been coming to Doc for two weeks now, I do not have a clue if it works or not.

"No, not yet. I will. Bruh, stop harassing me," I said, wanting to change the topic.

"I was just asking. By the way, how is your mom doing?" Sean said.

"Sometimes she seems to be okay. Then, other times she does not. She hasn't really been the same since she fell down the steps." I replied. While I was at the retreat, my mother was supposed to meet up with my brother. When she did not show up, he became worried. He had become even more worried when he wasn't able to get her on the phone. Come to find out, she had fallen. I received a call from my brother in the middle of the night saying mama had fallen down the basement stairs and was being taken to the hospital. She was in and out of consciousness. Worried, I jumped on my motorcycle and drove as fast, and safely, as I could back to St. Louis. My mother was in Mercy Hospital for two weeks. Now, she is in rehab for her hip, back, and neck pain. The doctors say she will be in rehab for a few months.

"You should get her in to see Doc when her therapy is done. It will probably be better if you had her seeing Doc while going to the therapist. It might speed her recovery along." Sean suggested.

"That sounds like an awesome idea, man, but my mom is not going to be a willing participant. I had suggested it to her right after I started my care. She told me I needed to be careful going to those kind of doctors." I replied.

"That does not surprise me that that was her response. She has been told by her M.D. to fear the chiropractor. Just keep trying. She needs it more than she realizes. Hopefully, she comes around. She will love it once she does." Sean said.

"I know. I will figure something out. I do not like seeing my mother all weak and dependent." I said.

"Keep your head up, Stephen. I promise, things will get better. Eventually, she will come around." Sean said, "Well look man, I am hungry and everyone is starting to arrive at the restaurant. I will have to talk to you later."

"Alright, Sean. I will talk to you later." Just before he hung up, I quickly added, "And tell Kelly I said Hello."

Just then, movement on the parking lot caught my eye. From where I was sitting, I could see the parking lot very well. When I recognized Kelly sitting in the car that had just parked, my heart began to race. I was so excited, yet nervous, that I had to remind myself to stay calm. She appeared to be talking on the phone. I figured she would be in the car a little while. So, I will sit here and wait for her to come in.

Doc's assistant was sitting at the front desk. He had just guided a patient towards the back office where the presentation was being held. As Kelly approached the door, I jogged the short distance from my seat to the door. I got there just in time to hold the door open for her. Her head was down, so she never noticed that I was the one holding the door open for her.

Chapter 27:   Kelly

"Well, mom, I will have to talk to you later. I have made it to Doc's office for the new patient workshop." I had just pulled into the parking lot of Doc's office. It was only seven weeks ago, when I first met Doc. Seven weeks ago, you could not have convinced me that I would become a chiropractic patient. However, seven weeks ago, I did not know what I now know about chiropractic and the benefits. A couple of weeks after the retreat, I finally made the decision to see her. It only made me wish I had not waited so long to get into her office. "Mama, you need to come see her yourself." My mom was always complaining about something hurting, but as soon as I mention chiropractic, she swears she is fine and don't need a chiropractor.

"Girl, I feel fine. I don't have any aches or pains. I'll see her when I do," she said. Then, she tried to start a new conversation. Every time I try to convince her to come see Doc, she always start a new conversation. "Did I tell you about your cousin? She called me today."

I did not have the time or the desire to argue today about why she should come to the chiropractor. So, I simply said, "Ok, ma. Talk to you later. Love ya!" My mother thinks she can heal everything, and believes pain is a part of aging. She calls it "growing pains". Really, now? Just thinking about it makes me chuckle. I cut the engine to the car, grabbed my purse out of the front passenger seat, and set it in my lap. I left the key in the engine to keep talking to my through my Bluetooth while my mom tried to keep me on the phone. "Mom, I am hanging up now. I will talk to you later." Reluctantly, she said she will talk to me later, and ended the call. I zipped my coat up, and tied my scarf around my neck before getting out of the car. The wind was whipping tonight. I just wish I had remembered to grab my satin lined hat, but I left it on the coat rack at home in my haste to leave.

Briskly, with my head down in the wind, I walked to the entrance of the office building. As I stepped in front of the door, it swung open before I could reach out for the handle. I was slightly startled, but grateful to be able to run right into the building and out of the cold air.

Never looking up, I thanked the person who had opened the door and proceeded to walk into the office. However, hearing my name stopped me in my tracks.

"Hello, Kelly. How have you been?" the voice said.

I turned to see who owned of the voice. I did not immediately recognize the gentleman, but when I did, I smiled. It was Stephen from the retreat. "Well, hello to you. I have been well. How have you been?" I had not heard from him since he abruptly left the retreat. I had hoped to hear from him after I had left my number with Sean. When I didn't, I had assumed that either Sean had not given it to him or Stephen had not been seriously interested in me.

"I've been good. I see you have become a patient of Doc's. You must have gotten a lot out of that weekend and realized you needed care. I know I did." He said.

Trying to make sure my face did not reflect the thoughts in my head, I smiled, and said, "Perhaps not right away, but shortly thereafter, I did give Doc a try." I looked away from him briefly, and then back at him. "Well, I guess I will go in and find my seat."

"Kelly, it is really good to see you," he said. Then, after a pause, he followed with, "Are you free after this workshop? I would love to have dinner with you tonight."

Blushing, I smiled, and said, "Yes. I'll join you for dinner." Yeah, my feelings had been hurt when I did not hear from him after the retreat, but I can ask why I had not heard from him during dinner. If I find his answer to be satisfactory, I may be able to forgive him. Hearing Doc starting the presentation, I walked ahead of him to find my seat.

Chapter 28: Stephen

When Kelly turned away to walk towards a seat in the waiting room, the receptionist saw me pump my fist in the air. He nodded his head approvingly. I was one happy man at that moment. I could not wait for this welcome thing to start and finish. I just wanted to hurry up and be with Kelly. I barely heard anything Doc said. The presentation was supposed to only be an hour. Yet, I wanted Doc to hurry up every chance she got.

An hour later, Kelly and I were walking out of Doc's office together. "Where do you want to eat?" I asked her.

Of course, she answered, I don't know. Women never know what they want for dinner. I should have known better than to ask her.

"Do you like Mexican food?" I asked her. Since she said yes, I knew exactly where I was going to take her. My favorite restaurant used to be Las Margaritas in Crestwood, but they closed a couple of years back. So, now, I go to El Maguey's. "Follow me to the Loop. I will treat you to El Maguey's. Have you ever eaten there?" I said while grabbing her hand as she stepped off of the curb.

"I've heard of it, but have yet to eat there." She answered. It was settled then. I walked her over to her car and made sure she was settled in before I walked over to my car. She waited patiently while I started my car and pulled out of the parking spot. She, then, pulled out behind me when I drove past her car.

It took us about ten minutes to get to the restaurant. We had to park a couple of blocks down from the restaurant, because that is where the free parking is. Since it was in the middle of the week, it was not difficult to find parking next to one another. When she pulled her car into the spot next to me, I could see she was on the phone. I wonder to whom she was speaking. Was she telling them about me? She got out of the car and came around to the front of mine.

"Did you lock your doors?" I asked her. I do not want anything to happen to her car or anything taken from her car because the alarm was not on.

"Yes. Thanks!" she answered.

We were silent as we walked the first few steps. Speaking for myself, I was silent because I was unsure what to say. Fortunately, I didn't have to figure it out either. She broke the silence.

"Stephen, I want to make a confession", she said. *Already?* I thought to myself.

"What is that?" I answered.

"I did not think I would hear from you again. I was kind of hurt when I learned you had left the retreat without us exchanging numbers. I really enjoyed being with you, and thought the feeling was mutual. So, I was disappointed when I did not hear from you during the weeks that followed, knowing I had given Sean my number to give to you. I figured you were not really interested in me", she admitted.

I never really thought about how she felt. I was so focused on my short comings and insecurities that I did not think about her feelings. I hate that I had led her on to think I was not very interested in her. In fact, that was farthest from how I felt. I left the retreat that weekend feeling hopeful and excited because in my heart, I felt I had met my wife.

"My sincerest apologies. I never meant to make you feel that way. I really enjoyed being with you that weekend. Although, I never reached out to you, I thought about you every day. Honestly, I was scared to reach out because I was battling an insecurity, which was making me doubt that you would want to be with me. There were many days I had picked up the phone to call. There many days I had dialed all of the numbers, except the last one, because I was scared", I confessed .

As we stood at the stoplight waiting for it to turn green, she turned to me and said, "I do not understand. You wanted to talk to me but you couldn't? What is this insecurity?"

I took a deep breath before I answered, "Well, last year, I had been in an accident. After the accident, I had issues with getting and maintaining an erection. Although, I can offer you everything else in a man, I was not certain that I would be able to please you. Sex is just as important as other things in a marriage."

We had started walking again when she said, "Marriage?!"

"I meant to say 'in a relationship'." I was nervous to know what she thought about all that I had said. Would she no longer be interested in being with me? "Well?" I asked.

By now, we had made it to the restaurant. I held the door open for her, while she walked through. "Well, what?" she asked.

"How do you feel about what I have said? Is it a deal breaker? Does that make me updateable?" I asked. I needed to know up front before we invested a lot of time into this relationship.

At El Maguey's, you select your own table and then a server will come take your order. I wanted to be as secluded as possible with Kelly. First, I went to the back corner of the restaurant near the bathroom. There is only one table back there. However, that table was already occupied. So, I took her back up to the front where there was a table near the front window. It was the second best table for us. After we sat down, she answered, "I do not know. I honestly cannot answer that question tonight."

"Fair enough. I will change the subject." I said. I had an anxious feeling in my chest. I really hope she says that her feelings are unchanged. I really, really like her. We ended up talking and laughing until the restaurant closed. It was as if we did not want to leave each other. I know I surely did not want to leave her. I loved looking at her when she spoke. Her whole face lights up when she speaks. She is so passionate and expressive.

Naughtily, I began wondering how does that passion translates in the bedroom. Her lips look very soft and kissable. I imagined sucking on them. As my thoughts went further and further south, I felt a stirring in my loins. Was it just me or was it getting hotter in this restaurant? While saying something, which I could not tell you what, she touched my hand softly but briefly. That slight touch tipped the scales for me. My pants had grown tighter between legs. Oh, shit! I have an erection! Yes! Dammit, it works, it works, it works! Hell yeah! It is on. I am coming for my baby! She does not even know what is on the horizon for her.

"Excuse me! We have to close the doors, now", said the waiter, breaking into my thoughts.

"Oh, no problem. We are leaving, now." I got up from the table and awkwardly walked to the cash register to pay the bill. I was one happy man. It was a good thing I was wearing black jeans, and the lighting in the restaurant was sort of dim.

When I had returned to the table, Kelly was standing next to it, waiting patiently for me. She is so beautiful. I want to love her for the rest of our lives. I grabbed her jacket from her hands, and motioned for her to turn around so I can help her into her jacket.

"Thank you," she said politely.

With her back to me, I could not resist the temptation to hug her. I moved in close and held her from behind. "Thank you for such a wonderful evening. I promise not to ever having you wondering where I stand with you. I hope you will eventually forgive me for taking too long to reach out to you." My cheek on hers, I felt her cheeks give way to a smile.

"I have already forgiven you", she said. At that moment, the Monster decided to greet her himself. He pressed into her back before I could pull back from her. I glanced at her from the corner of my eye. The look in her eyes told me she felt it. I gave her a crooked smile and led the way to the door.

"Let's get you to the car. I have already kept you out late enough." I said. After the Monster made his appearance tonight, my confidence returned. I pulled her to me and wrapped my arm around her shoulder. Now, that I had her, I was not going to let her go again. On the walk back to the car, all the lights were green, making our trip way to short. Our cars were the only cars in that part of the parking lot; a little privacy.

I walked her to the driver side of her car and waited for her to get in. Once she was in, I leaned inside the car, placing my face just inches from hers. My eyes locked in on hers before I kissed her like this might be the last time I ever saw her again. When I pulled away, her eyes were still closed and her lips were puckered. Oh, yeah, she wants more of that. Not tonight. Not tonight. Instead, I whispered to her, "Be safe getting home. I will call you in about twenty minutes to see if you have made it home." Her eyes fluttered at the sound of my voice.

"Ok," was all she could muster   .

Feeling myself, I walked away from her car with a smile on my face. I was back baby! The upside to this evening, the Monster was alive. The downside, I was going to have to tame the Monster myself tonight.

February

Epilogue: Sean

"Hey! Have you decided on what you will do for Valentine's Day?" I asked Stephen. He and Kelly had been dating since December, and will be celebrating their first Valentine's Day together. They actually make a very nice couple if you ask me. They really complement each other well. I have not ever seen Sean this happy about anyone he was dating. It is a good look on him.

"I was thinking that we will go to the event that Doc is hosting; that Couples Fusion event. It seems like a great way to set the mood for the rest of the weekend. I'm planning to make this weekend THE weekend. I have planned every detail I could possibly plan; from the wine to the music to, of course, the location", he answered. This year, Valentine's Day will fall on a Saturday, but Couples Fusion will be on Friday.

"Ah, yeah? Lisa and I are planning to attend that event as well." I added.

"Have you all attended this event before? What happens at this event?" Stephen asked. I explained to him that the couple will receive an adjustment, a couples' massage, and a slow movement core class that helps to set the mood. I told him it was like pre-four play, if that is even a thing. I also told him it was very nice, and assured him that he and Kelly will enjoy it.

"Not to be too nosey, but um, you and Lisa are still having sex while she is pregnant?" he asked.

"Man, yes! And, that is all that I am going to say." We shared a laugh. Then, I heard Lisa walking into the house. I had been missing her all day, and wanted to go see about her. So, I ended my call with Stephen, and put the cordless phone on the charger. While Lisa checked the mail on the counter, I approached her from behind and kissed her on her neck to let her know I was missing her. The mail was no longer interesting to her. She turned around to face me, and returned the love. She will look through the mail later.

Made in the USA
Lexington, KY
18 May 2019